FAMILY
RULES

FAMILY RULES

Teresa Taylor

ABSOLUTELY AMAZING eBOOKS

ABSOLUTELY AMAZING eBOOKS

Published by Whiz Bang LLC, 926 Truman Avenue, Key West, Florida 33040, USA.

For information contact:
Publisher@AbsolutelyAmazingEbooks.com

ISBN-13: 978-1945772283 (Absolutely Amazing Ebooks)
ISBN-10: 194577228X

For Bob again, my best proofreader, my no-holds-barred critic, and my endless inspiration. He is the one who makes me laugh when what seems like catastrophe has taken over.

The members of North Fork Writers' Group also deserve a sincere thank you, for their steady interest in writing and their devotion to the work.

Other Absolutely Amazing eBooks by Teresa Taylor

Family Matters

FAMILY RULES

FOREWORD

If in your reading you recognize some of the characters in *Family Rules*, it will be because you have already read *Family Matters*. But be assured these are not the same people whose lives you read about in the story of a young woman's perilous marriage and the family that tried to protect her. Years have passed, and they are all drastically different, in personalities, adventures and fates. Time has changed them, their circumstances, and their author in ways that will stun, startle and shock you.

- Teresa Taylor
November 2016

1

I used to think my Uncle Frank would protect me from my ex-husband. Even if – or *especially* if - he had to kill him. I don't think that anymore. I look over my shoulder no matter where I am, and in my moments of terror, I know I cannot rely on the one man I thought I could count on.

What unnerves me now every night is opening my apartment door. Usually I enter in safety and smile at my unrest. This particular night, my fears are confirmed. I am not two steps into the apartment before I know my ex has been here. It isn't anything I can see, it isn't an odor, it's more like a frequency in the air, the presence of a slight wind when no windows are open.

The idea that my ex-husband, who has beaten and raped me, has gotten access to my apartment, is unfathomable. When I recall our last time together two years ago, the tears, the promises of vengeance, the threats, the fury when I faced him to say it was over, my blood goes cold. I turn to lock the door and then, weak-kneed, I lean back against it.

"Easy," I soothe myself. "It's all in your head." I reach for that curtain of denial but it rolls back up, out of my grasp. "Get real," I tell myself. "He's been here and you know it."

There's a painted wood table in the corner just inside the apartment door. I drop my purse and books there, my usual first move to unburden myself of the day's work. On Fridays especially, I need to put the work aside for a while. As much as I love "my girls," East Harlem Academy takes every ounce of my energy, every day.

A quick survey reveals nothing unusual. It's still a spacious room with an old but polished wood floor, windows on two sides that admit considerable light, and very little furniture on the worn oriental rug that my grandmother left when she died. There are no indentations in the couch cushions, no empty dishes on the coffee table. The roll top on the old desk is down, as I left it.

I turn the corner into the kitchen. The window is locked as always. The cabinet doors are closed, the round glass table clean with only a philodendron on its center, the heart-shaped leaves leaning a few inches out of the ceramic bowl onto the table. The drain board next to the sink is empty, except for a clean wine glass. I stare at it. I know, I am *positive,* I washed it and returned it to the cupboard last night. I pick it up by the stem and hold it against the light, turning it to look for moisture or fingerprints.

"You're being paranoid," I say to the kitchen walls, just as a drop of water rolls out of the glass. It leaves a blot on my jacket sleeve. I put the glass down and back away as if I expect it to explode in my hand. Suddenly I need air. I lean over to reach the window. I unlock it, open it a few inches to let the early November air in. The air is still fresh but smells like dry leaves. I gulp a breath, my heart pounding. I pull the pane back down to the sill and re-lock it.

"Nothing but a wet glass. Get a grip." I lift the glass again by the stem and examine its bowl. No streaks, no prints. It isn't being very helpful, this conversation with myself. When I look down at the wet spot on my sleeve, the watermark is nearly invisible, drying fast. Can he really somehow have found his way back? He's been forced from my life by my uncle, and I have felt secure and protected for the last two years.

Can he have broken into the apartment? I had the locks changed long ago, on both the entry door to the brownstone and the door to my own third floor apartment. The windows are high and well secured. I am sure that no one can get in. True, I have recurring dreams at night that leave me shattered, but my days leave me no time to be afraid. Besides, he cannot come back. He is supposed to be in Las Vegas, working for Uncle Frank. I am counting on that.

Hands a bit shaky, I remove my scarf as I reach the bedroom, and toss it on the bed. I look slowly, carefully around the room, my breath rapid. Nothing unusual flags my attention as I step out of my skirt, slide my arms out of my jacket, and turn to hang both items in the closet.

My hand freezes in midair. There are no clothes on the rack. No skirts, trousers, jeans, blouses. My entire wardrobe seems to have disappeared. Unbelieving, I run my hand over the bar on which my clothing should hang. Nothing. Not even hangers. As my glance shifts to the closet floor, I stifle a cry. A pile of jumbled fabric lies there, flung amidst the shoes and boots. I kneel, grasping for a logical explanation for their presence. Has there been an earthquake? A rumbling truck that shook the house? But I know, even as I reach for a solution, that my speculations are ridiculous. The mess in front of me has nothing to do with events outside the apartment.

I lift a lavender silk blouse from the floor. It has been slashed repeatedly, leaving a fringe of silken fabric hanging from my fingers. Holding it closer, looking at it more carefully, I imagine I can feel the waves of anger still vibrating from it.

Terror forms a lump in my gut, traveling from my stomach up to my throat. Dizzy, I take two quick steps into the bathroom and vomit my lunch into the toilet. Leaning back against the cabinet next to the bathtub, I realize a string of lavender silk is still hanging from one of my fingers. I shake it loose as if it's a scorpion. My balance still a beat off, I catch myself from falling into the tub. In a moment's horror, I re-live the day Joseph pushed me violently into the tub, where the slam against the wall had fractured my clavicle. It still hurts.

My whole body shakes as I make my way back to the closet. Kneeling again, I pull the crumpled nest of clothing into the light and separate items one from another. Almost every piece has a slash, a rip, or a hole. Several are unpleasantly wet and freshly stained. I won't allow myself to question how they came to be in that condition.

I am in trouble. I know where I need to turn for help. But I resist bringing my uncle into the picture. "Not happening," I say aloud. "Bring Uncle Frank into it, I'll never get my life back." I feel immediately guilty. I have to face the truth that he'd gotten me out of a ruined marriage two years ago, rescued me from a puzzling nightmare I couldn't solve myself, rescued me from three years of sexual and emotional abuse that left me beaten and broken.

At the time I was hysterically grateful for the plan my uncle invented for my safety. To get my husband out of my life and under his direction, he created a job for Joseph in Las Vegas, a job offer Joseph couldn't, and didn't dare, refuse. I was grateful, thinking I would have my life back when he was gone. It did not occur to me then that my uncle's grip on my situation would revert to what it had always been in the past – intrusive, controlling and all-knowing, not to mention dangerous. Grateful or not, I remain aware that I'd given up my independence and control of my life once he'd taken on his role of rescuer.

What I live in fear of is the power with which he has accomplished all this. My uncle is someone to reckon with, a man whose word has changed (or shortened) the lives of many.

My phone buzzes. Trembling, I walk back into the living room and fumble in the purse I've left on the entry table. The buzz ends just as I retrieve the phone. I am in no shape to have a conversation, not with anybody, but curiosity and fear overcome me. I click to access the message. At the same time, I recognize the incoming number. It's all too familiar. The message is brief, and not typical of my uncle, who normally leaves no message. "We have to talk."

The crazy part of my mind takes charge. "He knows," I mutter. "He knows I need him. He can smell my fear. I'm going to have to call him back."

2

My uncle is sitting at his usual table, his back to the wall. Fearful as I am about leaving the house on this late Saturday morning, he has assured me of my safety and insisted I meet him at Café Blue. It is a long block distant from my apartment in Fort Green, and I look over my shoulder with every step. But it is our regular place when he comes to my neighborhood, just as Nunzio's is our spot when I meet him in Bay Ridge. I sit across from him.

"Look like you swallowed a snake," he says.

I whisper, eyeing the woman reading a magazine in the corner two tables over. "That's how I feel. I told you, he was in my house."

"Not possible," he says. He sips his espresso. "I was calling to tell you he was in town; he was with me almost all day."

"He messed up my closet, took a razor to almost every piece of clothing I own!"

"He came into town night before last, he stayed in the city with Sal Terranova. No way he got anywhere near you."

I am starting to feel more helpless than I was the afternoon before, when I was alone in my apartment with clear evidence that someone had been present. "You're not listening to me. My clothes are destroyed and there's no explanation? What am I supposed to do to convince you?"

I wait a beat. No response. "Where is he now?" My voice rises in frustration and anger. The woman in the corner turns her head, then discreetly looks away.

My uncle checks his watch. "Airport," he says. "Leaves

for Vegas in an hour."

I put my coffee cup down hard. "You're making me question my sanity. And yours."

He gives me a glance that could freeze soup. "Okay," he says. "Let's say someone got in the apartment. Made a mess. Anything stolen?"

"No, I don't think so."

"So somebody vandalized the place. Some local, maybe. Came in through the roof vent or something." He shrugs to show his frustration. "I can't make it any clearer, it couldn't have been him. He's doing a lot of work for me, has things under control out there, gets paid big time...I don't see him risking that."

We're both quiet. I search my mind for a better way to present my case. Nothing materializes.

"Which brings us to the reason I called you," he says. He adjusts his sparkling white shirt cuffs, avoiding my gaze. "Just wanted to let you know. He'll be back next week. For the next few weeks, he's running a project for me here."

I lean forward in my chair. "Here? In New York?" I've raised my voice again. The reading woman closes her magazine, folds it into a cylinder, and gets up to leave.

My uncle watches her go and checks his watch again. "That's what I said. Take it easy, we'll keep an eye on things. You'll be okay."

But *why*?"

"Because he's the person for the job."

"I can't believe you're doing this." My hands are shaking.

He gives me an icy level look. "You don't question my job. Or my decisions. You know that. You're part of this family and you know the rules." He looks at me more closely. "So stop with the tears."

I wipe my eyes. I'm not getting anywhere with this. My uncle obviously has a plan and I know what he invests in his

8

work. He will continue to deny the story I've told him. But I can't give up.

"How am I going to feel safe?" I demand. "You promised to protect me. I don't feel protected." I gulp, trying not to cry. "I never thought that wouldn't be your first priority."

"I'll send one of the guys today. Check the weak spots, the locks, maybe repair something." He looks away. "We'll figure it out. You'll be fine." He rises from his seat, kisses my cheek. "Trust me. I got your back." He has not even asked to see the damaged clothing. I know he doesn't want to climb three flights of stairs, but that doesn't seem a good enough reason.

3

After a long and chilly walk through Fort Greene Park, I head reluctantly toward home. Every stretch of street looks ominous, every person sinister, every alley a trap. Even a man carrying a toddler shakes me to the core when he catches my eye and wishes me a good afternoon. I walk blocks of pointless detour to avoid the possibility of running into him again.

It's getting dark. With nowhere else to go, I manage to climb the stairs to my apartment, but I'm terrified to open the door. The key in my hand trembles to the point that it wouldn't fit it in the lock. While I'm still struggling with it, my phone buzzes.

It's my uncle. "Just giving you a heads-up. Guy's coming over in a half hour to install a brace lock on your door. Waste of time, really, but it'll make you feel better, okay?" And he hangs up.

Ten seconds later, the phone buzzes again. "Forgot to tell you, his name's Vinny. You okay?" He waits through five seconds of my silence and speaks again. "Katherine, you hear me? This work for you? I don't want to send him all the way over there and you're not home."

"I'm home," I say quietly, having managed to unlock the door and let myself into my own living room. "Thank you," I speak into the phone and hit the off button. There is nothing I can say to him that would make any sense at this point.

With the phone still in my hand, I call Erin. My best friend, she's an artist and a designer, a bit flaky on occasion, but capable of analyzing a situation with brilliance. Living in Boston near her stepdad, she makes sure we keep in close touch. She's still the only woman I can confide in. I think of the times at Loreto I've counted on her for advice (usually crazy) and comfort (always effective). They resonate clearly in my memory, even though some of the situations have occurred five or more years ago, when we were still foolish trusting college girls.

She answers on the second ring. "It's Saturday evening. Don't tell me you're home alone." Her voice carries humor like a light breeze.

"Yep," I answer. "I'm home, and not planning to go out. Not ever again."

"What *are* you talking about? Was that last guy a loser? Are you giving up men?" She sounds interested, or at least involved.

I recite my story. She remains very still for about five seconds, which for her is a major power outage. Then, "You want to come up here for a week or two?" she says.

"Oh, Erin, I can't. My job's full time, the school needs me, I have an extra class on Monday... But I'm scared. Not sure what to do. Uncle Frank seems to think I'm delusional, although he's sending a guy over to install an extra lock."

"Well, we both know you're not nuts. Want me to come there?"

"No! I've got to handle this. Just not sure yet how."

"Do you think you need a gun? I know some people..."

I am struck silent for so long, she begins to laugh. "Okay, okay, sorry I asked. I know, I forgot your family's in the whatever-kind-you-need business." Even I have to smile. At that moment the downstairs doorbell rings. I freeze.

Erin hears it. "Go. Answer it. Don't hang up. I'll be listening."

I open the door just a crack. "Yes?" I call.

12

"Vincent here. Your uncle sent me."

"Come up," I call. "Third floor." It's loud enough for Erin to hear.

"Okay," she says, "give me a call as soon as he's gone." Still somewhat hesitant to lose her, I disconnect.

4

Vincent is trouble on the hoof, way too handsome for his own good, and he acts the part. Muscled up, cut-off sleeves, deliciously masculine perfume. Brown curls slightly suggest the need for a haircut. Magnetic green eyes hold mine for a split second too long. He looks me up and down as if he is going to get paid by the inch.

"My uncle said your name is Vinny."

"What does your uncle know about my name? I prefer Vincent."

He gives the living room and me a casual survey. "So you're the brunette in distress," he says. He puts a metal toolbox on the painted table inside the door. "Show me what happened. Where'd the guy get in?"

"How should I know?" I say. "I came home and he'd been here. Somebody drank from my glass, messed up my clothes closet."

"Where's the closet?" he says, walking toward the bedroom.

I feel strangely humiliated. There is no chance I'm going to show him the condition of my empty wardrobe, the ragged fabrics in a pool on the floor. "No! Stop," I say.

He gives me a crooked look. "Look, I don't go into everybody's bedroom. Good-looking as you are, I don't want anything from you but a look at the crime scene."

"You can't – I mean, I don't want you to see..."

Now he looks hard and carefully at my face. "I get it. He did something disgusting, right? Like dirty your stuff."

I nod, starting to sniffle a little.

"I'm really sorry to push it. I'll just check the room. You can close the closet door if you like. And you have nothing to be ashamed of."

"Wait here," I say. I get on my knees in the bedroom, scoop the pile of ruined clothing into a travel bag. I stuff it into the back of the closet, and close the door. "Okay," I say over my shoulder.

He walks in like he lives there. Surveys corners, ceiling, molding, windows. He looks in my direction out of the corner of his eye and laughs. "You can get up now."

Still on my knees in front of the closet, I start to scramble to my feet. "I was just –"

"Yeah, yeah, I know. I make you weak in the knees. Happens all the time." He opens the closet door and examines the ceiling inside. "Just what I thought. Got a step ladder?"

I point to the utility closet in the corner, where the washer and dryer stand. He moves the ladder to the clothes closet and when he climbs its two steps, his head and shoulders disappear into a darkened corner. "Get me my toolbox," he directs me.

The box weighs more than I can comfortably manage, but I haul it into the bedroom. He reaches down for it. "Gonna make some noise here," he says. "Just so you're prepared," and his head and shoulders disappear again. I hear hammering and shrieking wood as he curses mildly on his perch.

I can't see anything, and I can't stand there admiring his denim-clad lower torso. I retreat back into the kitchen and put water on to boil, just to have something to do. I'm not even sure what that would be. Should I make tea? Coffee? Ramen noodles? I'm suddenly hungry at the thought. A glance at the clock tells me why. I've eaten nothing all day but the two delicate cookies that had come with my coffee at Café Blue, many hours ago. Besides, doing

16

anything at the stove is brain therapy for me, even something as simple as ramen noodles.

I chop an onion and throw it with some butter and olive oil into a well-worn cast iron pan. I watch it start to sizzle and lower the heat, leaving the onions to soften. I take a couple of garlic cloves out of the basket on the counter and add them, along with a pinch of dried thyme and a few red pepper flakes. I cut a chunk of parmesan from the cheese drawer of the fridge and grate a pyramid shaped pile of it on a sheet of waxed paper. When I have more than I need, I wipe my mother's four-sided grater, cleaning the remaining cheese crumbs from its inside, where the cheese crumbs are likely to collect. I am starting to relax.

This is going to be an upgraded ramen noodle meal. Nervous, I realize as I stir the pan's ingredients that I am counting on Vincent's presence at my table. I swallow my anxiety, picturing us sitting at the kitchen table, talking about my uncle or discussing favorite foods. Maybe I really *am* delusional, as my uncle suggests.

The water is starting to boil. *Why ramen noodles?* I ask myself. That has been my fall-back emergency meal when I get home too late and tired to prepare real food. I reach for an opened box of linguine off the pantry shelf. What the hell. I've already boiled water. Why not cook the real thing?

I'm about to put the handful of linguine into the boiling pot when the phone rings. I lower the heat to simmer. It's Erin. "You okay? You were going to call me when he left. He can't still be there, can he?"

Holding the phone to my ear, I take two shallow bowls from the cabinet and place them on the table. "Um. Yeah, doing some work on the closet ceiling. He must have found something wrong."

"You feel safe? Is he okay? How long you think he'll stay?"

I fish two forks and spoons from a disorganized drawer,

and place them next to the bowls. "I think he's okay," I say. "I feel safe. He found a problem and started to fix it. Shouldn't be much longer."

Behind me I hear his voice. "I'm done but I still have to install the brace lock, remember?" He looks at the table and inhales the contents of the iron pan. "Smells great. We eating before or after the lock job?"

Erin raises her voice. "You still there? Did I hear something about eating?"

"No, no. I think, um, I think he said something about the heating system. Listen, I have to go. He needs to start on the lock, so I'll have to hold the door for him. Talk to you soon."

I click off and turn to face him. He gives me that per-inch look again before he speaks. "I didn't say anything about heating," he says. "But you know that, right?"

I nod. "It's an old friend. She sometimes makes a big deal about things, so I didn't want to explain..."

"Explain what? That you made dinner for a perfect stranger?"

I shrug. "Why don't you install the lock, and we'll talk about dinner afterwards."

It takes him about fifteen minutes to attach the brace bar to the door and then bolt it to the floor. I have already reduced the heat under the slightly simmering water. He comes into the kitchen and starts putting tools back in the metal box. Finally, he looks at me. "You're good. Safe as Fort Knox," he says.

"What did you do in the closet?"

"There was a rotten board that's part of the attic floor. I thought it might have had something to do with the break-in, but the roof wasn't affected. So I just replaced the board." He places the last tool into the toolbox. "No big deal."

I turn slightly to bring the water to boiling again and

face him. "Thank you," I say.

"Give me your phone for a minute, please," he gestures to my cell phone on the kitchen counter.

"Sure." I hand it over.

Eyes fixed on the screen, he pushes a few buttons on his own phone and then slowly puts my phone back in my hand. "Thanks," he says and starts to leave the kitchen.

"What did you - Why did you want my phone?" I stumble over the words.

He looks at me hard. "I don't like women who lie, especially to their friends," he says. "But I wanted to have your phone number, in case I change my mind about you. Make sure you lock the door behind me," he says, and leaves.

I listen to his footsteps all the way down the three flights. Something in me prays he will come back up. But he doesn't.

In the kitchen, I put the linguine back in the box and throw the ramen noodles in the now boiling water. I know they'll take only two minutes to soften. I'll mix them with the buttery onion sauce, and then I can decide if I have enough appetite to eat.

5

Sleep eludes me. Well, why wouldn't it? Within twenty-four hours of being terrified out of my ability to think straight, I have cooked for an attractive man I don't even know, have hoped to share a meal with him, and been rejected in the most humiliating conversation ever. Sleep? I feel more like throwing myself in front of the train at the Lafayette Avenue station on the corner.

Obviously, the fear that comes of having my apartment vandalized, and the conviction that my ex-husband is responsible, has left me feeling incredibly vulnerable. My uncle's denial that Joseph could have been in the apartment is testing my trust beyond imagination. I have for some time been coping with my lonely existence, but suddenly it seems not only sad but unbearable.

My thoughts go back in time nearly a year to Cliff, the college friend to whom I'd turned for entertainment and attention at first, while I was still entranced with my untrustworthy husband-to-be. Cliff had pursued me single mindedly, and I had deflected his pursuit but clung selfishly to his good company.

Cliff became an indispensable and loyal companion when my relationship with my family had become worrisome, and we continued our friendship later, after graduation, and after Joseph had been removed from my life by my uncle.

I thought of Cliff as my security blanket and savior. Admittedly, I took advantage of his comfort. When Erin moved to Boston to be near her stepdad, Cliff became the 'girlfriend' I needed, the person I could call at any hour, meet for lunch in the city on a bad day, the person I could spend hours with, watching inane TV together. He made me laugh when I wanted to cry, wiped my tears when the laughter failed.

"You're like a brother, a father, and a therapist, all in one." I said often.

His role as caregiver after I'd been left alone had gone on for several months. I expected the attention and coddling to last forever...until the night I was feeling adolescently sorry for myself, and the tears started. Cliff was sitting next to me on the couch, and he reached as usual for my hand. Suddenly he leaned close and began to lick my tears. Gently, he kissed my temple, then my cheek. He whispered something I barely heard, and I turned my head, where his lips met mine.

I started to pull away, but the kiss continued. His breath was sweet and warm, and I drank it as if I'd never tasted sweetness before. He ran his hands across my breasts, caressed my throat and gently laid me down on the cushions.

"I've been waiting for this a long time," he murmured, moving his hands into my hair. I moved back a little, moaning a whispered "No." But his other hand reached down to my skirt, sliding it up as he pulled my panties down. He looked deep into my eyes. He moved his lips without sound. "Is it all right? Are you ready?"

"I –I'm not sure. I don't think, I wasn't thinking of this..."

"It's just a lovely gift," he said, "for both of us." Then, "You're so wet," his voice caught roughly. And we pushed forward together as he moved into my body, a body that welcomed this long awaited feeling of being taken and used with pleasure. I cried when I came, just for the release, and the recognition of something I'd thought was gone from my life.

"Are you all right?" he said, rearranging my hair. "Are you happy?"

"Cliff, I'm fine, but I feel so...so strange." I had trouble finding the words that would work. "As if I'd fucked my brother. Or my father."

"I'm neither of those. Is that a problem for you?"

"I need to think about it," I said. What I needed to think about was my own callous treatment of him. I had never considered him in a romantic light. I had rejected him time after time, alternating between anger and selfish ego satisfaction when he clearly wanted more. In short, I had acted like a slut.

We sat for some minutes more. He was very quiet. I couldn't find the words to explain this sudden rift I saw growing between us. It hurt me. But my mind couldn't get past the role he'd been playing for months, the role of comforter and healer, a role of neutrality, not one of passion.

"It's getting late," I finally said. Guilt stuck in my throat.

"I'll call you tomorrow," he said. "Don't forget to lock the door." And he was gone.

For me, it was the beginning of the end of a friendship I had cherished. I blamed myself for submitting to his love making. But I felt taken advantage of, too. The brat in me was enraged. This had not been part of our deal, and now I felt obligated to change the nature of the roles we had accepted.

The sex had been delicious, but I'd never contemplated a romantic relationship, and now Cliff would expect his long-sought dream to come true. I couldn't accept that, and I wasn't having it. He'd start again with his protective behavior, which I associated with my uncle's intrusive control, that mind-numbing sense of dependency I'd tolerated for years. I vowed to free myself from Cliff's

23

concern and care.

I remember calling Erin that night and hysterically telling her what had occurred.

"So you two got it on," she said. "So what? He's kind, handsome, and he's crazy about you. Always has been. What's your problem?"

Still crying, I choked out an answer. "We didn't have that kind of relationship. Promised each other to stay friends. For years. Since college, when he was the one who listened to me, backed me up... I feel like he betrayed me," I said.

She was silent for ten seconds. "The one? I seem to recall listening to you, and backing you up, too."

I heard the hurt in her voice. "Don't go there," I said. "I didn't mean it like that; of course you were my support in every way. It's just that he was a guy..."

"Gotcha." She laughed that chuckle that used to stop conversation in mid-stream. "I knew I could change the subject if I tried hard enough. Look. You're being ridiculously hard on him, and on yourself. A guy like him fucks me, all I can say is thank you!"

"I know what you mean. But I can't think of him that way. I feel like I did it with my brother or something."

She sighed. "Think of him however you want. Don't turn your back on a good thing. Hey, it's midnight. Talk tomorrow." She disconnected, and I said 'Okay" into the dead phone.

Now that I look back on it, I was incredibly cruel to him. When he tried to contact me, I disregarded the call. I erased the fervent messages, the pleas for discussion, the promises of atonement. I was a bitch. I recalled one afternoon when he intercepted me outside East Harlem Academy. In his suit, his hair seriously making him look like a young Robert Redford, he was the banker's son he'd been raised to be.

His actual presence made him hard to ignore. "Why are

24

you here?" I said. As if I didn't know.

"You are destroying me." That was all he said. I felt compelled to answer. Holding my pile of books and briefcase, I sat on the low stone wall that bordered the path to the school's entrance. He sat next to me.

"Cliff, I love you in my own way. You have been my solid and staunch friend for several years. That was the role we both played. But everything changed when–"

"I know. I jumped the fence. I was – am – so crazy about you, there was no other way to show it."

"It was a valuable friendship. You took care of me, protected me, and I'm grateful. But, Cliff, it's over." I remained strong. "I can't be the woman you want. I never saw you as a romantic partner, and you were well aware of that. Think of all the times we had harsh words about my feelings for Joseph, argued over your wish to save me. We were just *friends*!"

I started to cry as the full impact of my loss struck me. "And now we've betrayed that."

Things have never been the same. I discourage his visits still, assuring him I am recovering from the bitter end of my marriage, lying that I am coping well and not in need of friendly help. At the same time, I am furious with myself for throwing away the friendship that has kept me functioning for so long, and half admitting to myself that the sex I am missing had been wonderful.

Cliff's calls have tapered off. On the two occasions I actually answered his call, he was distant and cool. "Hope things are going well," he said during the first conversation. "Let me know if you need anything."

The second call left me bereft. He did the usual "Just checking in" routine and then ended the call. "I guess you don't really need anything I can give you," he said. Something about that broke my heart. It was the last call from him for a long time.

6

The early December dark is announcing itself earlier every day. The second floor light bulb is out, but the stairs to the apartment feel less like a climb than most days, and the shadows don't reflect my mood. Even though I am physically exhausted, my back pack feels light this Friday afternoon. I'm thinking of my girls at the Academy, and still smiling at my memories of the day. They are so smart, and so willing, and their recent progress has been amazing. I hug my pile of books a bit tighter, eager to start reading their latest submissions.

Turning the last landing, I hear a strange sound, a soft whisper it sounds like, and I stop short. I cannot see the stairs above me without beginning to climb them, and I have no intention of doing so. Quietly, I put my books on the landing and bend to disengage the back pack from my shoulder. As I lean forward, I hear it again.

"Welcome home."

Panicked, I turn to retreat down the stairs. I don't descend one step before I feel a hand grip my upper arm.

"Where you heading? I could've sworn you were on your way up." I can't miss the familiar mocking tone in his voice, the voice right next to my ear. It's Joseph.

"What are you doing here?" I whisper, fearful of raising his anger. I use some force to pull my arm away from his hand, and he releases me so suddenly, I lose my footing, one leg turning slightly under me. He puts his hands on me again, steadying me on two feet. Like a striking serpent, he snatches my bag from the bottom step, and throws it to the top of the stairs. He turns me toward the apartment and begins to push me up the last flight.

"Stop asking stupid questions," he says. "Just move."

"I'll scream," I say.

"Great idea," he says. "Neighbors aren't home yet. I checked. I wanted to be sure we could talk without disturbing anyone."

I pull in whatever direction I think will free me. He's behind me and shoving me with all his strength toward the apartment, one hand on my back, the other arm around my waist. I dig my nails into his hands and he laughs. I reach backward to scratch his face and he grabs a handful of hair. Mistakenly secure, I have let it grow to my shoulders, and he has no trouble using the clump of dark hair to steer me in his intended direction.

At the top, he pushes my bag into my hands. "Open it," he gestures to the door, still holding a hand on my waist. Hesitant to obey his command, I don't move. He pushes me hard against the door. "Do it," he says. "I'm *not* going to talk to you out here in the hall."

Trembling, I fish the key from its compartment in my more or less organized purse. As I struggle with it, unable to insert the key neatly into the lock, Joseph begins to laugh.

"Can't get it in, huh?" He whispers in my ear. "No worries. I'll show you how *I* can get it in when we're inside." His breath is in my ear. "But first, give me the damn thing." He removes it from my shaking fingers and turns it in the lock. He turns the knob, but the door doesn't give.

"What the fuck," he curses. I drop my purse as he pushes me harder into the door, this time slightly twisting my arm up behind my back. I have not felt terror like this since we were still living together, when I was holding my breath every waking moment, and previewing every word that came out of my mouth. He takes my wrist gently, and I gasp in pain as he raises my arm higher. "So there's another key?"

I hold tears back with effort. "Yes, in my purse. Another key."

"Why not on this ring?" He removes the used key from the lock.

"I haven't had a chance. It's new. I didn't have time –"

"Just like you, not to be prepared. It's like always; you need a lesson." He reaches for the purse on the floor and puts his hand inside. "Nothing's ever easy with you." He locates the key to the brace lock, shoves it into the lock, and pushes open the door.

He walks me over to the couch and sits me down. Moving deliberately, he walks back to the door and takes a few steps to gather up my dropped belongings. I look cautiously around, realizing that without my bag, I have no phone.

He turns suddenly. "Don't even think about it," he says. "I want you where I put you." In seconds, he is back in the apartment, both locks secure, my books and papers stashed on top of the old roll top desk. He continues to hold my keys.

It is actually the first time I am able to look at him since he trapped me on the stairs. To my shame, my initial thought was that he was still good looking as ever. The man has always had the ability to catch a woman's eye, and now he stands before me, damn handsome and magnetic as ever, his gorgeously tan skin a shade or two darker from the Las Vegas desert sun.

"So. How's it going?" He sits next to me on the couch, his hand on the back of my neck. "Great to see you, Kit." He surveys the room from corner to corner. "Still living here by yourself?"

I move away, ignoring his question. "You broke into my home," I say. "How'd you get in here? I know it was you. But how?"

He laughs, sliding his hand forward, under my chin.

"Kit, what makes you think it was me? Anybody could've picked that piece-of-shit lock."

"No one else would've done what you did." I breathe, aware of my vulnerable position, trying to gain control. "Joseph, I want you to leave. You don't belong here. Get out."

"Now, don't be bitter. Makes you look ugly." He scans my body from the floor up. "But right now, you're looking good." He smoothes my skirt, making sure to push his fingers between my legs, and feels the silky fabric of my shirt. "Nice rags. Look new. Guess you've been shopping, huh?"

His mocking tone makes me want to puke. He *knows* I have been forced to buy new clothes and he is enjoying my discomfort and fear.

What am I going to do? The neighbors are conveniently absent. I knew they were away. They'd asked me to keep an eye on things for the next few days. He must've watched their schedules. The thought makes me cringe. He's obviously been in the neighborhood more than once. It's over three weeks since he broke into my home, destroying my sense of safety and privacy, taking up residence in my entire being. Now he sits in my apartment, perfectly at ease, and I am without phone, resources or help.

"How did you get into the building?" I ask for the second time.

"I know people with keys," he says. "Have to admit I missed the new lock, but here we are anyhow, right? And now, I've got the new key." He smiled, swinging the key rings around on his fingers.

He's enjoying this. Eyes focused on some distant image, he keeps talking. "You know, people will believe anything if you tell the right story." He makes himself more comfortable on the couch. "The folks downstairs, they believed the paper I put in their box, asking them to confirm

30

the date for resuming paper delivery." His self-satisfaction shows in his face. "So, you and me, we've got some time together ahead of us. Plenty of time to take care of things."

"What things? Things were settled a long time ago. My uncle –"

He laughs aloud. "Your uncle! Your uncle could give a shit. He's dealing with some difficult folks right now, and counting on me to fix the problem. That's where he thinks I am now, solving his problem, which I'll do later. All he cares about me is that I can do it. You may be on his mind, but you're pretty far down on the list at the moment. Sure, he's concerned with family, but sorry to disappoint you, Cinderella, you are number ten on his top five. So, back to taking care of things..."

I am reassured by the calm and sober tone he maintains. I speak calmly. "What do you want from me? What is it you want to 'take care' of? We're legally divorced, you signed the papers, we're done."

"It may feel like that to you, but I'm not done. I *had* to sign those papers at the time. Frank was still reminding me about my new position with him, how rich he was going to make me, how you were a part of my past not worth remembering. He worked at distracting me, got me three Las Vegas bitches who'd do anything I wanted. And they did."

He shakes his head in mock disbelief at his good fortune. "They were so good, you can't imagine. They did things for me I didn't know I wanted. I thought I'd forget you. I *tried* to forget you. Just didn't work. You were that juicy little girl, that innocent college girl who knew how to please me, who was afraid not to."

He runs his fingers through my hair, gently at first, then winds a thick strand around his hand. He pulls me slowly closer. I resist out of instinct but the pressure and my memory remind me I can't win. "Stop," I whisper. "Please stop. I won't fight."

"See what I mean? You *want* to please me. I know it." He leans back a little, loosening his grip. "Left that shiny dark hair long for me, huh?"

I swallow the knot of terror in my throat. I remind myself he can be swayed, if I appeal to his ego, his insecurity. Had I been able to get my hands on a weapon, I could have, would have, killed him. But I move closer. "I understand you've got some issues to resolve with me. I know our separation was not a mutual decision. Not at first, anyway."

"For damn sure. You got me snatched away before I could even say 'So long,' before I could even screw you one more time, have a last leisurely fuck with you. You know, Babe, that hurt me most of all, not having you one more time."

I am dead quiet. Is this what he came for, is this what was going to happen, now? What ammunition can I use to dissuade him, to calm him, to satisfy him, other than to give him the thing he seems to want most. The thought of sex with him makes me cringe. I don't trust his strength, his emotional extremes, his possible lack of control.

"So this is the plan," he says, relaxing back into the couch cushions. "We figure out how we can get back together. I manage to get back from Vegas once a month, we shack up for a few days every time, you and me, live like the old days."

"Joseph, you're dreaming. The 'old days' disappeared a long time ago. There was a reason my uncle got you out of town –" My mistake. I sense the blow before I see it or feel it. It's a flat slap in the face but there's enough action behind it to snap my neck.

He leans over me, turning my head toward him. "Don't bring up that bullshit," he spits. "That was another time, I was another person. So were you. We were *good* together."

32

Obviously, he is building a dream, but I don't think it's safe to say so. His expression grows soft, his eyes focus on some memory I can't imagine. "Good together," he repeats.

I have to somehow change his mood. "Let me get you something to eat," I say, attempting to rise from my seat. "It's five o'clock. Maybe some soup, or a sandwich..."

He turns to me, his eyes betraying the invented memories he has fallen into. "See? You still care. I knew it." His voice falls to a whisper. "My pretty little college girl, willing to do it all for me." He stands up and bends toward me. I flinch. He whispers as he lifts me from the couch. "Don't be spooked. I won't hurt you."

He looks at my face, at the red splotch on my cheek. "That wasn't me," he says, caressing the spot with the hand that doesn't support me. "Just one of those things. You know what I mean, don't you? You know me better than anybody, you know I can't hurt you."

He is carrying me into the bedroom, still murmuring words I can't hear, don't understand. I try again to shift the mood. "Please, let's not think about the past," I say. "Let's talk a bit, take care of those things you want to settle." I look straight into his eyes. They are still soft, tender. He is somewhere in his head. "Maybe we can make a plan," I say. I am desperate, but I know better than to struggle.

He places me on the bed, careful to ease me down. "This *is* my plan," he says. He unbuttons my trousers and pulls them off, puts his finger into the elastic of my panties and slides them down to my toes and then to the floor. He doesn't bother with my suit jacket and blouse.

He stands next to the bed for a moment, looking down at me as he removes his jeans and briefs. "This is what I've been waiting for," he says, kneeling over me, his erection in his hand. "And," he enters me slowly, "it was worth waiting for." I close my eyes, hoping he won't hurt me. It does hurt, but in ways I have not expected. I successfully fight my instinct to cry.

7

It is late into the evening. The apartment is dark. I am alone and naked in my bed, listening to Joseph's footsteps in the kitchen. I roll quietly over, tip-toe into the bathroom, and turn on the shower.

In a second, he is next to me. "Trying to wash me out of your life?" He shakes his head. "It's not going to work."

I move around him to step into the running water. He watches me scrub myself, tears already sliding down my face as I relive what has just occurred. He hands me a towel from the rack and walks out of the bathroom. The water has gotten very hot. I turn it off, and dry myself as tenderly as I can, sensitive to the soreness of my ill-used body.

I hear him open the refrigerator door, recognize the scrape of a drawer opening, the thud as the door is slammed shut. "Hey," he calls. "I'm making a sandwich. Want one?"

"No." I grab my jeans and a sweater from the closet and pull them on. I find my "teacher" clothes on the floor, the neat little J Crew trousers and blazer I'd bought after my wardrobe had been sabotaged. I hang them in the closet, hoping the wrinkles will shake out. The blouse will need washing, for obvious reasons.

I walk into the kitchen. He is smearing mayo on a slice of wheat bread. A couple of layers of cheese and a slice of ripe tomato are already piled on another slice of bread, which he then covers with the first slice.

Looking me over, he begins to eat. "How come you dressed?" He chews a bite of his sandwich. "Aren't you ready for the next round?"

He must see the blood drain from my face. "It's okay, Kit, it's okay. Those couple of fucks were so sweet, I just have to have you again. Just one time, I promise." He smiles and takes another bite of his sandwich. "Let's do a quickie and then I promise I'll leave. I promise."

I have heard his promises before, too many times to even think he might live up to them. I start to walk past him, into the living room where I know my phone is in my purse.

In a second, he is blocking my way, pushing me back toward the kitchen. At the same time, he snatches my purse from where he's left it with my school books on the desk. He turns it upside down on the kitchen table, and finds my phone among the items that fall out. I realize he still has my keys. Vincent has left me copies, but I can't recall where I've put them. I'll turn the place upside down later.

He puts the phone in his pocket. "I'll just hold it for you until I leave," he says. "You're not going to call the cops, are you?"

He knows I won't. I've been through that before. In the past, he came across all soft spoken and professional when they arrived. He'd say I was his wife, we were having a harmless difference of agreement, and they'd give us a brief lecture before they left. If he says the same thing now, how can I prove otherwise? I'd never changed my last name, not even when I married him, so any records they check will reveal me then and now, still as Katherine Gabrielli.

"No," I say. "I'm not going to call the police. But I can tell you now, the locks won't be the same for long. And I am going to fill my uncle in on everything that you've done here."

He laughs, showing me both keys as he puts them into his pocket. "Including the fuck?"

"You mean 'the rape,' don't you?"

"I didn't see you fight me off."

"Never did me any good before," I say, remembering

the brutal last days of our marriage.

He looks at the clock. It's Saturday morning already, a few minutes after two a.m. "Got an appointment later on tonight," he says. I know most of his so-called appointments have to do with women, drugs, or jobs my uncle gives him. Sometimes it's a combination of all three. I hope he'll be in a hurry to leave, but the clock means little to him. On the other hand, he does check the time, and curses about the urgency of his task.

In the bedroom, he handcuffs me to the headboard. "Want to make sure you'll be safe while you're waiting for me to come back. Be just a little while. I know you'll miss me. See you in the morning, for sure. After I make copies of your keys." He is already yanking my sweater over my head. I hope he'll leave my phone behind and I realize I can't reach it if he does.

Well," he says, "let's get to it." I pray that he really means 'quickie,' as he's promised. I pray I'll survive the morning, knowing he'll be back to keep his promise.

8

"**O**kay, okay. I'm sending Vinny over Monday to replace the locks. You say he got into your apartment?" Uncle Frank seems impatient and rushed, preoccupied. I hear voices in the background. I have no idea where he is on this Saturday morning.

I try to keep the phone call simple. "Actually, he got into the building, and then he waited for me on the stairs. He took my purse and used my keys to get into the apartment."

"Did he hurt you? You okay?"

"He was rough. He took advantage of me. He got in as I was coming home from school yesterday, and left this morning. He took my phone, but gave it back before he left. He got what he wanted, which was to control me." There is a tremor in my voice. I don't mention that he stayed for hours, alternately threatening me, handcuffing me, and taking his time to rape me several times before he left.

My uncle's voice softens. "Look, I'll take care of it. He should know better than to even show up there. He's doing so much work for me, I think it affects his thinking." He growls a deep chuckle. "You won't see him again, I can guarantee."

"But you've said that before. He just does whatever he wants and thinks he'll get over..."

"I'll have a talk with him. It's what – almost noon. I'm going to meet him in a half hour. We're driving out to the Hamptons, I'll have plenty of time to explain things to him. Believe me, I won't have to tell him twice. You're my niece,

I take care of you. He's riding the wrong horse. Not for long, trust me. Besides, he's heading back to Vegas tomorrow. That make you feel better?"

I take a deep breath, my voice shaking. "Do you think Vincent can come sooner? I'm afraid. I've got the regular apartment key, but I have no key to the brace lock, he took the keys with him. I have to go to work Monday, and I'm afraid to leave the apartment with only one lock secured." I am lying. Joseph has left all the keys, relying on the copies he made. I just want Vincent to come. Now.

"Okay, I'll connect with Vinny, he'll come tomorrow. I'll have to bribe him to work on Sunday, but I'll make sure you get what you need. That make you feel better?"

"Thanks, Uncle Frank. I appreciate it. I didn't want to bother you, but he was, he was so..."

"Listen," he says. "I got it, it's going to be okay. He's got to know this can't be happening, and I'll make sure he does. Understand?"

I nod into the phone, unable to get past the tears and make myself heard.

"Understand?" He repeats. "I'll take care of it. I'll take care of you. We'll have dinner together tomorrow at your Aunt Mary's, okay? I'll send Vinny early so you'll have time. Get some family stuff going, and you'll feel better. Okay?"

I sniffle a weak "Yes." He hangs up. He is blowing the whole story off, treating me like a hysterical woman who needs soothing. It isn't like him. I think back to the fury he'd shown when he found out I was being abused by my husband. This is the uncle who'd once threatened to "make him disappear." Now he is going to "have a talk" with him. I do not feel safer.

9

"You have got to be kidding me, changing your locks twice in one week. What the hell is going on? What made you think I work on a Saturday?" Vincent stands at the apartment door, tool box in hand, looking like a cop who's about to give me a ticket.

"Thank you for coming today. My uncle said you'd be here tomorrow."

"Yeah, well, it sounded important. So what happened?"

"Not my fault," I say. "Really."

"Okay, what happened? Tell me the story. The real one." He sounds almost patient. In the living room, he removes his jacket and throws it on the couch. I sneak a look at those ridiculous upper arms, momentarily distracted.

"Okay," he says. "You don't want to tell me. Let me guess. You were fooling around with the keys and they broke in the locks. Happens all the time with women." Scorn drips like oil of vitriol from the last word.

"Please," I say. I sit in the desk chair. "Don't treat me like an idiot. Or a child. I was forced to give the keys up when my former husband surprised me in the stairway. When he left he took the keys with him to make copies. That was yesterday and I am really afraid he'll try to get in...again."

"So you think he was the guy the first time?"

I nod.

"Sick fuck. Excuse my language, but he sounds like a psycho." He goes through the tool box, selecting things he needs. He turns and makes eye contact. "I'm going to make you safe. The place'll be like Fort Knox." He hesitates. "Guess I said that last time," he says. "Didn't help much, huh?" The eye contact continues. I feel nailed to the chair. He turns back to his tools. "We may have to put a land mine in the downstairs foyer, maybe a fingerprint checker."

He gives me a quick look. "You can smile now."

I blush. "Thank you. I know you'll make the place secure. I'll just have to be careful coming home..."

"You have a gun?"

I cringe. "No."

He digs further into the tool box, and comes out with a dainty-looking pistol. For a moment, I think it's a toy. It's pink. "Here," he says, putting it on the desktop in front of me. "It's a Ruger SR22, and it's loaded. Gave it to my last girlfriend, but I took it back when she pointed it at me. I'll show you later what to do with it. And don't shake your head at me. If you really want to feel safe, it's the only way."

I don't touch it. There is no way I am keeping a gun in my apartment, much less knowing what to do with it. He starts working on the locks and I watch, mesmerized and paralyzed. He works rapidly, removing the new "old" locks and installing the two he'd brought with him. Finally, "Okay, we're good."

I stand up, avoiding contact with the gun on the desk. He surveys the room. "Where do you keep your jewelry?"

"In the bedroom."

He gestures in that direction. "Come with me, bring the gun with you."

"No way I'm touching that thing."

He breathes an exasperated sigh. "Okay, I've got it," he says, lifting it carefully and heading for my bedroom. I cannot help but follow him.

"Let me guess," he says. "In a box, in the closet."

"Yes."

"Top shelf, right?"

"Yes."

"Okay, get it, I'll show you where to put it."

I stumble over my best boots, stretch up to take down the box, a carved wood case about the size of a shoebox. He takes it out of my hands and opens it. There are two shelves, one above the other. My things are on the top shelf. He examines my small collection of necklaces, my larger collection of earrings, a few good pieces left by my dead mother. He raises the shelf and looks at the empty section below.

"Nice," he says. "Don't panic, I'm not touching anything. Just checking you have room for Ginger." He puts the gun on the bed carefully. "Well, that was her name before. You can name her whatever you want. But it's good to give her a title. Makes it easier to make her your friend."

"Look, I don't want a gun, I can't use it, and I don't need another friend."

He ignores me and walks into the laundry closet, a niche in the corner of the bedroom. Above the washer is a shelf, holding two gallon jugs of organic detergent. Next to the shelf is a small cabinet, which he opens. "Uh-huh," he moves things around, talking to himself as he checks the inventory. "Clothes iron, stain remover...Perfect."

He turns and goes back into the bedroom. I follow like a puppy. I have lost most of my resistance. What if I do need a weapon at some point? I might as well be prepared. If Ginger can protect me, why not get to know her? I am already thinking of her as a person, a security guard to share my apartment.

He sits on the bed, and pulls me down next to him. "This is what you need to know." He shows me twice how to unload the pistol, and then load it again. He watches me as I try to copy his moves. It requires six careful, terrified, painful attempts before he takes my hand and smacks it with his palm. "Gimme five," he laughs. "You got it!"

He removes Ginger from my hand, and installs her gently in the bottom shelf of the jewelry box, avoiding any disturbance to the pieces on top. "This goes up in the cabinet," he gestures toward the laundry closet. "One of the last places anybody'll look. And if you hear someone coming, you have time to retrieve it. Normally, I'd say keep the ammo somewhere else, but the situation you're in, you should leave it ready and loaded. But don't touch it otherwise, hear me?"

He gets up off the bed and heads for the door. I follow. We stop in the living room. He packs his tools. At the door, he turns. "Okay, no more lock changes, right?" I nod.

"Good. Next time you see me, I'll be coming up the stairs to pick you up. We're going to get Ginger registered, and pay a visit to a shooting range I know. I'll call you first."

He leans toward me and I think he's going to kiss me. Instead, he brushes some dust that has fallen from the closet and landed on my chest and shoulder. I back up slightly. "One more swipe," he says, brushing both breasts, and then he's out the door and whistling as he plunges down the stairs.

10

Forty Sixth Street looks like a tributary of the East River. The water sloshes from pools that traffic can barely navigate, and comes up over the curbs, leaving the sidewalks inches deep in water as the rain whips through the tunnels of Manhattan side streets. I close my umbrella, now useless in the wind and saturated anyway, the fabric drenched so completely that it appears to be raining from within.

Wet to the knees, I crane my neck to look up the block for Erin. A stupid move, really, since visibility is nothing but a concept at this point. I back into the theater's entrance and let the water drip off me as if I were a garden statue with a recycling shower.

"Here I am," she says from behind me. "Swam all the way from the subway." I turn, thrilled to have found my best pal. She's as drenched as I am, and still shedding drops in the lobby.

"And right on time for a change," I say.

"Couldn't help myself. Amtrak got here on time so all I had to do was wander over from Penn Station. Otherwise I could definitely have been late, to meet your expectations."

We hug. "I am so glad to see you." I pull the tickets from a damp pocket. "I've been wanting to see *Book of Mormon* since it opened. When did we buy those tickets? Last year?"

"Honey, it was probably right after they opened, but my memory doesn't go back that far." She pauses for a second. "I can't remember anything these days. I really think I'm approaching senility."

"Erin! You're – we're – what? Twenty-six? Maybe what you mean is you don't *want* to remember some things. But that's my gig, not yours." When she shrugs and produces a half smile, I continue. "I'm the one who's always trying to forget." We're suddenly being swept into the theater by a crowd that smells like a rainy-day dog.

"Tell you what," she says. "Let's go in and see the show, and we can talk later. I want to hear the whole story. Stories." She laughs. "I think you gave me every gory detail by text and phone, but there's nothing I'd rather do than make faces at you while you talk. I want the details of Joseph's invasion, and Vincent the Hunk, or was it Hulk, and I think you mentioned someone named Ginger." She pauses. "Ginger... Yeah, who is this Ginger?"

By this time we're being shown down the aisle to our seats. "Oh," I say, "she's like my sidekick. Tell you later." We settle ourselves, put our umbrellas on the floor, and sit, ready to be amused.

~ ~~

The rain has stopped and the drains have swallowed the worst of the floods. Skirting puddles all the way down Fifth Avenue, we find the Lebanese restaurant Erin has insisted we try. The room is spacious, with wooden beams on the high ceiling that reaches the second story, where there is a mezzanine. Despite the rain, the windows shed light on the downstairs tables, where we declare one for ourselves.

"Hope the food's good as the décor," Erin mutters, shaking her raincoat and hanging it on the back of a nearby chair. The waitress hustles over to whisk both coats to a corner behind the cashier. "I'll give you ladies time to dry off. Back in a minute," she says, placing menus on the table.

We are already seated when I realize I have left my umbrella in the theatre. "Just like you." Erin rolls her eyes and focuses on the menu. "We can go back and try to recover it later. I think you did that the last time I came, when I made that long trip from Boston just to get caught in the rain."

"Not my fault," I say.

"It's never your fault. I'm starving. Let's order."

"My cheek muscles hurt from laughing," she says, over a kale salad that show-cases three shrimp as décor. "Just that line about the maggots..." She starts giggling again, and sips her sauvignon blanc.

I swipe my pita bread in the bowl of fresh hummus and take a bite. "Yeah, random but hilarious. It was worth the price, outrageous as *that* was. They should've delivered those tickets on black velvet!" I join her in a laugh.

"Okay," she suddenly gets serious. "Let's get to the main course. Start talking. Tell me what's been going on." She sips her wine again, and I inhale a substantial swallow from mine before I launch into my tale, the whole soap opera revolving mostly around Joseph's invasion of my home and his subsequent abuse. I drop a sentence or two about Vincent's lock repairs, and his somewhat personal gestures of advice. I never mention the gun.

When I am done, she shrugs. "It figures," she says, almost to herself. There's something in her tone that sends a message. The trick is to translate it. She is holding something back, and I know her too well to ignore the obvious.

"What?" I say.

She doesn't answer.

"What?" I ask again. "C'mon," I urge. "You're making me nervous. What's up?"

She taps a manicured finger on her wine glass. "I don't want to creep you out, but..."

"But what?"

"Now, don't panic, and I could be wrong, but..."

"Erin!" I almost scream. "Spit it out. Now."

"Okay, okay. When I was waiting in the theater lobby,

before you showed up, I thought I saw Joseph waiting outside. He held a dark blue umbrella that partially covered his face, and it was raining so hard I couldn't be sure. But I got the creepiest feeling I wasn't wrong."

Watching my face, she puts her hand across the table to touch my arm. "Then you came in to the lobby, and when I looked again, I didn't see the umbrella anymore. So maybe I made a mistake. But I kept seeing it in my mind, just a part of his face, the open umbrella, the rain..."

I am almost relieved as I run her story through my data bank. Finally, I draw a deep breath. "Listen, I'm glad you told me, but I think you can forget it. As far as I know, he's back in Las Vegas, and last I heard, he was running special deals for Uncle Frank. Believe me, if that's true, he hasn't got time for stalking."

"If that's true," she repeats.

I change the subject. "Let's order another round," I say. "Neither one of us is driving," I smile. Smiling is an effort, but I pull it off and catch the server's eye. "Two more, please," I point to the empties.

Within a few minutes, the waitress approaches with the two wine glasses on a round tray. In her other hand, she is holding an umbrella. She leans the umbrella against an empty chair, while she places the glasses carefully in front of us.

"I think I have good news for you," she smiles, as she bends to pick up the umbrella. "Is this yours?" She holds it up for both of us to examine.

For a moment, I can't process what's happening. "Why yes, that looks like mine," I say, recognizing the rose pattern and the pink tape ribbon that binds it closed. "Where did you get it?"

"A gentleman stopped in just a few minutes ago. He said he'd picked it up in the theater under your seat and, when he caught a glimpse of you on the street, thought you might be the person who left it." She hands it over to me and smiles broadly. "One of the things I love about this city, sometimes it's like a small town."

She notes the shocked confusion on my face and senses I need reassurance. "He was a very nice gentleman," she says. "And easy to look at. One of those tall, dark and handsome types, you know? Anyway, I'm glad you got it back." She turns away. "Enjoy your drinks," she says.

Erin stares at me. "He followed us. And not from Las Vegas," she says.

11

Our trip back to my apartment is unusually quiet. We can't seem to find the words we need that will comfort one another. The R train clatters along, providing background noise that covers our silence.

We get off at DeKalb Avenue and start a slow walk up the avenue. The rain has reduced itself to mild spitting. Finally, Erin speaks, shoving her umbrella into her tote bag. "What are you going to do?"

"Haven't got a clue. Last time I took this issue to Uncle Frank, he blew me off like dust. Joseph says my uncle's too busy to be bothered with me, but I think there's something else going on."

"What could be going on? He's still your uncle, and I remember him when he'd follow you to the ice cream store to insure your safety. And," she laughs, "you were nineteen years old!"

"Let's forget my uncle. I have to deal with this myself, or with help. But whose help?"

"What about Cliff? You know he'd come riding to your side like a knight on horseback."

"Not possible. I hurt him too much after that last time. I wouldn't answer the phone, acted like a bitch ... He's probably got me on his blocked-call list."

"What about the cute locksmith guy?"

"Erin, he *works* for my uncle! Getting around that could be a storm of trouble. I know Uncle Frank too well to have to trust Vincent."

"Yeah, and you'd be responsible if something bad happened to him."

I nod. We are in front of the brownstone and take one last survey of the street before we unlock the front door and start the climb to the third floor.

Vincent is sitting on the first landing. "Hey," he says. He does his usual body survey, top to bottom and back again. "I was tired of sitting outside," he says. "Too wet. So I let myself in." I start to say 'how' and cut it short. He is, after all, a locksmith.

He stands and puts his hand out for Erin to shake. "Nice to meet you. I'm Vincent." She nods, speechless for a change.

He turns to me. "Don't look at me funny. I could have let myself into the apartment. But I didn't."

So far I haven't spoken. I stutter. "Wh- what are you doing here?"

"Well, I was coming to hang out with you and Ginger. But I see that's not going to work today." He leans over and kisses me hard on the lips, and raises a hand to Erin. "See you again sometime," he waves, and rattles down the stairs and out the front door.

"WTF?" Erin looks at me as if she's my mother and I've come home at four in the morning. "I think I've been run over. Where'd he get those eyes? And who is Ginger? And why would you be 'hanging out' with her and this hunk?" She narrows her gaze. "Are you into threesomes with him?"

I start to laugh. "You always think the worst and sickest thing first. Come on up and I'll fill in the blanks."

"Yeah," she says, one step ahead of me. "And you'll connect the dots, too, I bet." Sarcasm hangs sharp in the stairwell's dusty air as we make our way to the third floor. She turns back to look at me. "Kit, this better be good."

"I'll do my best." I start putting the ridiculous tale into a form she can accept. I still don't want to share the truth. Who would believe me, anyway? Until I get my reaction to Vincent straight in my own mind, I can't, *won't*, reveal anything as it has really happened.

12

Thanksgiving comes late that month. The November day is as gray as the sky above it, a dull wrinkled aluminum. On the elevated portion of the subway ride to Aunt Mary's house, I keep watching out the dirty window for snow flurries, but none appear. I recapture the wisp of a dream I had that morning, which had left me frightened. My uncle had played an odd role in it, and I hope I won't have to be part of any meaningful conversation with him. I put the thought away as the train screeches to a halt.

Outside Aunt Mary's house, there are no noticeable changes. The house is still one of the loveliest in the neighborhood. It reminds me of the family home in the TV series, *Blue Bloods*. The title refers now to a family of cops, but even when I was a child, the house always struck me as elegant and elite, bringing the name "Blue Bloods" to mind.

Inside, I welcome the warmth. I hang up my own coat, checking my surroundings as I always do at Aunt Mary's. The table is loaded like a pioneer's covered wagon, stacked and ready for whatever culinary onslaught might occur.

Aunts Concetta and Sarina sit on the sectional sofa, making comments about the food, mostly in English. They will soon be part of the onslaught. They speak in hushed tones about absent family members, mostly in Italian. This has been their way for years, gossiping in Italian, thinking to keep their secrets from me. But after all this time, I know exactly what they are saying. For their pleasure, I continue to pretend puzzlement or confusion.

I approach them for the customary hug and kiss,

babbling the required pointless remarks about their appearances and health. "Look at you, Kit," Concetta says. "Cute as ever. Maybe a few pounds more than last time I saw you." She glances at Sarina, whose bulk trumps us both. "Well, more to love. And by the way, is there a boyfriend in the picture? At your age – what are you now? 29?"

"I'm 26, Aunt Concetta. It's been two years since my marriage crashed. I'm not looking for another guy now, really."

Concetta takes my hand and touches my empty ring finger. "You've got to do something about this," she says. "Somewhere there's a guy with what you need – money, protection, love. There's a dozen guys connected with our family who'd put a diamond on that finger. The perfect accessory, if you know what I mean."

I gently remove my hand. No need to offend. "I'm not up for getting close to those people. Not in my lifetime."

"Don't get uppity," she says. "The business has done a lot for all of us. It's a corporation we can all count on. And it's not crazy like the old days, you know what I mean?"

"You mean since my parents were killed by suspects unknown? Because one of the family "friends" had a grudge to settle nine years ago?"

"Let's not go there," Concetta says. "You don't know as much as you think you do. This is not a proper conversation for Thanksgiving." She turns to Sarina with her eyebrows raised. "Luckily, Frank took Domenica to the Caribbean. Can you imagine if they were here – Let's shut that subject down, now."

I pretend to search in my purse for car keys I don't even own. I don't really want to pursue the death of my parents with either of these sisters. It would be a wasted conversation. The trust level is zero. I remember too clearly the day after Thanksgiving, some nine years ago. I was a freshman, a recent orphan, home from college for the

54

holiday. Concetta had taken me out to lunch, to inform me that my parents' house was being sold and my finances from here on would be handled by the family. "Family rules," she said in response to my confused questions. "You're too young to be on your own." She wasn't totally wrong, as time would tell.

Their spouses, Uncles Big Tony and Little Tony, are still standing by the frozen front window, in deep conversation. With the men, it's all about money and trouble, money and crime, or money. The money part is what matters. We all know it.

Just the same, things seem quieter than usual. I recognize after a moment the source of the emptiness, Uncle Frank's absence. It's like Thanksgiving without dinner, sort of. It feels strange.

Aunt Mary sees me as she comes out of the kitchen, carrying a tray of champagne glasses. She puts it down on the coffee table, and approaches me, her arms already open to give me the usual bear hug.

"Sweetheart, my only niece!" After the hug she does the pinched cheeks and the survey. "You look beautiful! Look at her – gorgeous face, lovely skin, like a model!" She demands the others' attention. "Just look at her, the only child from this whole family. Five sisters, and only one a mother. Can you believe that? Weren't we lucky the Gabriellis had her!" Then to me, "Have you lost weight? A little thin, maybe. Are you eating right? A good breakfast, every day?"

Bianca and Richie open the front door, Nina close behind them. It's perfect timing. The wind brings the gray day with them, but just for a moment. Nina swoops me into her arms before she even drops her coat. "You smell delicious," she says. "It's that patchouli stuff, isn't it? Don't tell me, I know it. Nobody smells like you."

Not much older than I, having just turned thirty, Nina still plays her role as youngest aunt, and I love it. I look into her face, cloudless and innocent as always. Her hair now is a blond curly halo. It is perhaps less striking than the lavender dye she sported all summer, but she always looks like an angel, regardless of her style of the moment. She has continued to live with Bianca after Bianca's marriage to Richie nearly three years ago. Somehow, the three of them manage what Nina calls a "spirit of familyness."

In so many ways, Nina reminds me of my mother, who had shared the same sense of adventure, the same inclination toward risk. She was older than Nina by over a dozen years when she died. I had been born into this family of secrets when she was just fifteen, something I did not know until after her death. The pregnancy had hastened her marriage to my father, who was not only young but half Irish on his mother's side, making him a questionable addition to the family. But Nicky Gabrielli passed the crucial tests when he started working for my uncle. And Giulia, his beautiful, radiant, pregnant bride, my mother, was thrilled.

I loosen my hug as Nina relinquishes me to Bianca. Aunt Bianca, second youngest of the sisters and still in her thirties, had been a source of support and advice during the hard times, without which I'd never have survived. It had started as advice to the lovelorn, when I realized Joseph was cheating on me. It ended with Bianca making sure Uncle Frank knew of the abuse I was suffering, a development which had changed everything, resulting in the temporary removal of Joseph from the east coast, and my new life as a divorced woman.

Bianca holds me now as close as she can, as if she's still protecting me from the trouble she'd helped me through when things were at their worst. Richie makes it a triangle hug, embracing both of us with genuine affection. The whole mood of the room changes.

Called to the table, we find our places and begin to pass

56

platters. The uncles and their wives have little to say, stacking the food on their plates and cramming it into their mouths, emitting grateful positive noises in between bites. Conversation is at a minimum until Aunt Mary speaks.

"What a break for Frank! Here we are in this freezing weather, and he took his girlfriend to Aruba. I hope they're having a good time without us." She sighs.

Big Tony swallows and frowns. "Well, we're having a good time without them."

Concetta uses her wifely voice. "Tony, what a thing to say. Sure, we're having a good time, but not because they're not here."

"Whatever. I didn't mean nothing." He fills his wine glass for the third time. It is generally advisable to avoid making snide comments about Frank, although I concluded he was just trying to compliment the chef.

Bianca chimes in. "Richie says Frank needed to get away for a few days. Right, Richie?"

She looks with affection at her husband of three years, and he pats her cheek. "Yeah, Frank needs a break. Too much going on, too many problems right now. Maybe it was too soon to start the Vegas project, after that last deal with the Atlantic City boys."

"Let's not –"

"Who says?"

"Which deal?"

The three senior sisters talk all at once, over voicing one another. Bianca and Nina remain still. The uncles look to Richie, who holds up his hands in the "don't shoot" position and calls for quiet. "We've got to be patient. Nobody has a good feel for what's happening next. But it doesn't pay to get in a twist over what hasn't happened yet...Am I right, or am I right?"

He turns to our matriarch, the beautiful Aunt Mary, her neatly coifed white hair enhancing her good looks. The eldest, and a widow, she is the accepted go-to person for opinions and problems. He is respectful. "Mary?"

"Nothing for us to discuss," she says. "Without Frank here, what's the point? We have to trust his judgment." She sips her wine. "Let's enjoy our dinner." She looks around the table and passes a bowl of sweet potatoes in my direction. "Kitty, have some more. You're a skinny little ragazza." She has called me *ragazza,* street urchin, as far back as I can remember.

The conversation brings me back to the nightmare I had that morning just before I woke up. I dreamed I was getting in the shower when I felt a hand on my back. Terrified, I turned to see my uncle. He was dressed in his usual attire, dark suit, crisp white shirt cuffs, shined shoes. He took a gun from his chest holster, and pointed it at my naked body. "Not to worry," he said. "I'm no worse than the rest of them, but I'll do what I can."

And as he backs out of the bathroom, I wake up. I lie still, my heart pounding and my hands sweating. What does it mean? Why him? What about pointing the gun at me? I have already begun to suspect he is a threat to me, and this seems to confirm it. But he didn't hurt me in the dream, and he told me not to worry.

"Kitty, the sweet potatoes! Hello?" It's Concetta, pushing the bowl nearer to me. "In your own world, huh?"

"Sorry, thinking of something else." Which is true. I had purposely tucked the dream away, hoping to deal with it another day. I am relieved and grateful that my uncle is not present. But he won't be gone forever. I curse inwardly as I put a potato on my plate.

Fucking damn. I know I might need his help. I received it once and it had saved my life, but I am starting not to trust him, and I am trying desperately to not only solve my own problems, but also to keep my distance from the family's web of loyalty.

I live with daily awareness of the power my uncle wields over them, playing his role as a puppet master for not just my aunts and their families, but for the connections he has outside their circle. I learned long ago he was a criminal and a business man, a person with no boundaries, no limits to the extent he would go to get what he wanted. I fear his motives. What if he needs Joseph more than he needs to protect me? Besides, I know he will own me completely if I depend solely on him for my safety.

I am still trying to retrieve the freedom I had once felt in the early days of my love for Joseph. In the end, he destroyed my will, my strength and my confidence, and returned two years after our divorce in the most terrifying manner, to vandalize my possessions, steal my sense of security, and rape me in my own home. I vow to someday become again the young woman I'd been after Joseph was gone: able to cope, do my job with pleasure and delight, and solve my problems without help or interference.

13

Two weeks later I sit with my uncle at Café Blue. We are opposite one another at the small round table he favors. I have broken my vow. It seems no longer possible to live the safe life I long for, after finding an envelope in the mailbox on a Sunday afternoon, my name written in curling red letters, no stamp and no address, clearly placed there by someone who'd gotten into the foyer that requires a key for entry.

"So you think he's stalking you?" My uncle chomps a bite of his croissant, brushing the crumbs off the table.

With shaking hands, I pass the letter across the table to him. I watch his face as he skims the text. I have memorized it already but it still seems like something that has been created for a horror movie. I need not read it; I have etched the message's words in my troubled mind.

You will never forget you are still my wife, and I will come back to you whenever I feel the need. Keep your legs open, because I want your pussy waiting for me when I want it.

My uncle looks up from the sheet of paper and hands it back to me. "Looks like a prank," he says. "Some asshole with a taste for babes like you. I'd tear it up and toss it."

"Uncle Frank, I am *not* a 'babe.' I have steady, professional work, I don't hang out in bars, I keep respectable hours. What kind of people do you think I know? Besides, whoever wrote this had access to the downstairs door. And I told you, I think he copied the key."

He considers his croissant for a moment, then looks

back at me. "Thought you said Vinny changed all the locks twice. Joseph couldn't have copied them the second time." He takes another bite of his pastry. Still chewing, he watches me while he speaks. "What I figure, either some jerk slid in behind one of the tenants, and left you his little love note, or - what do you think of this? - Vinny's fucking around with you. Or, he didn't change the downstairs lock."

"Vincent? Please, Uncle, we need to make sense out of this. What about the 'you're still my wife' line? Vincent wouldn't even know any of that. Would he?"

He wipes the last flaky crumbs from his lips and sips his coffee. "Ah, who knows what these guys know? Maybe Vinny talked to one of my guys and heard about the deal I made with Joseph, that he was safe as long as he took care of Vegas, and left you alone. So far, he's kept his side of the bargain, far as I know."

Now I am exasperated. He has *not* kept his bargain. But my uncle refuses to believe my stories. Also, there is no way Joseph would explain to anyone his residence in Las Vegas. His ego is too big to admit that his work there is part of some deal. But I can't convince my uncle. I am getting nowhere.

"Uncle Frank, do you know where he is, all the time?" I see the impatience in his eyes. "I'm just asking. Is it possible he tells you where he is but he's somewhere else?"

"He wouldn't do that. He knows he owes me. Owes me his life, if you want to put it that way. Look, I don't trust anybody, but the guy's reliable, even if I got to force myself to admit it. I mean, you know I don't like his type, but I got no complaints, and he gets the job done, sometimes better than anybody else. Hell, he knows what's going on better than the old timers. Can't ask more than that."

He pats my arm across the table. "You get what I'm saying? I don't believe he'd do this to me. He knows the stakes and he understands what we call 'family rules.' A roll in the hay with you can't be worth risking what he's got, even if you are my beautiful niece. He's got women everyplace he goes, know what I'm saying?"

I know exactly what he means, but it is clear he isn't worried as much about what happens to me, as he is about what might be done to him. Men and their egos.

14

Georgia Trent meets me at the schoolhouse door on Monday morning, turning the lock to let me in. She always manages to look both chic and professional in her pricey blazer and crisply ironed jeans. "Good morning, early bird," she says. "It's almost seven o'clock, you know."

"Thanks, Doctor Trent. One of these days, I'll get here late enough to open the door myself."

She gives me her most affectionate smile. "Yeah. You overachievers make my life hard," she says. "Next thing you know, you'll be taking over my job as Director."

"No chance," I say. "I like the girls too much to hide in an office." We are walking comfortably down the hall to my classroom.

"Oh, Honey! You know I love those young ladies. But that office has become my second home. I'm lucky they aren't charging me rent instead of paying my salary."

She stops walking as I approach my classroom. "Oh, almost forgot. Some gentleman was here late Friday, after you'd left. He was asking about your schedule, claimed to be from the Teacher's Union. Said you had filed a complaint."

She must see the expression on my face, and puts out a hand to soothe me. "Now, don't worry. I told him nothing, and told him to come back with the union representative, and the complaint papers in writing. It was obvious he was trying to pull off a scam of some kind; I mean, I know you have no complaints," She smiles before she adds, "I took his picture as he turned to leave. It just didn't smell right, you

65

know?"

"You took his picture. May I?"

She fishes for her phone in her jeans pocket. "Sure enough. May be hard to recognize. He had already started walking away when I caught him." She slides past a few pictures in her gallery, and passes the photo to me. "He didn't know I took it, I just raised my phone and hit the button. Printed it later in case I needed to deal with the authorities, or show it to you. So I have a copy if you want one."

She's right. It isn't easy to spot him, unless you know him. It's a full body picture. He is well dressed, obviously on a mission, and has turned away just as she took the photo. But I instantly know the turn of his shoulder, the arrogant angle of his head, the almost-visible profile.

"It's your ex, isn't it?" She puts her hand on my shoulder. "You've never told me much about him, but you conveyed more than you said. You know I will always protect you. And don't forget we have the two security guards at the doors."

"Were they there on Friday?"

"No. It was too late. They leave around 4:30, if all the girls are gone. They stay late only if there's some activity that keeps students here."

"So you were alone?"

"Yes. Everyone was gone. I was just making a few calls to parents. Always wait till after six, hoping I'll catch them home from work. Those who don't work nights."

We have often discussed the need for many of the parents to work two jobs. I nod to show my understanding. "Yes, and I was gone, but some days I stay late, too. Hard to believe he took the chance to show up here."

"He's likely not to do so again, since I made it quite clear there were roadblocks to his request. I think he caught on I didn't believe him."

"You handled it fine," I say. "We'll talk later." She deserves the reassurance. When Georgia walks away, I glance down the hall. The doors are unlocked now, and I need to get my material ready for class. I try to put the conversation behind me as I get immersed in the pleasure the students give me. But still, I find my hands shaking and my mind elsewhere as the first seventh grader walks in the door.

She finds me in whatever drawer I've been hiding my head. "Miss G, we having a quiz today? I studied real hard, and I'm ready." She gives me a brilliant smile.

"You mean '*really* hard, not *real*.' Remember about –"

She finishes the sentence for me. "Uh huh, we use an adverb to describe an adjective. I get it, I really do. It's just habit, and I have to change it. I even told my mom."

"You corrected your mom?" I hope she hasn't.

"Oh no, Ma'am, I'm way too polite to do that. Last year was my first class here, and I learned a lot about how to be polite with grownups."

"I'm impressed, Janina. You just absorb everything like a sponge!" I glance at my watch as half a dozen young women push each other through the doorway, still chattering their daily gossip. Behind them the remaining ten show up, shoving one another to avoid being last one in.

Somebody has to be. "Marta, could you please close the door, and I think we need more light today. Flip the right hand switch, if you don't mind."

Marta does as I ask, and looks at me for confirmation. "I got here on time today," she says in a low voice as she passes my desk. "Wasn't my fault I was the last one in."

"Of course not," I said. "You're right on time." Which is true. It has become a weird kind of competition this semester, that the last one be pointed out. I still am not sure exactly why it's so important to them. I have repeatedly explained that people generally come through a doorway one at a time, and someone therefore has to be last, but they cling to their female insistence that, in their game, it isn't quite right.

By this time, I am fully involved in their active work, as one group moves together to compare completed homework problems at a table in the back, and several others begin to write questions on the white board, listing the homework tasks that have given them some difficulty. The rest are at their desks, already opening to the editorial page for today's discussion of the New York Times letters about college loans.

My thoughts are totally tied up in theirs, no room for my terror or confusion about the visitor who asked Director Trent for my schedule. For another few hours, I am Miss G, who is ankle-deep in the job and the students she loves so much.

15

The subway is packed, a source of welcome distraction as I ride home. At each station, I entertain myself by taking note of the last one in. The students' obsession with this phenomenon has made me curious, and I keep track by judging those who get in last. There's the timid soul, usually an older woman, who can't brave the crowd, and waits till the last minute to find a way to squeeze in. There's the late arrival, the athletic young man who has flown down the stairs from the sidewalk, leaped over the turnstile, and pushed gasping into the nearest car, where he pretends to be reading the ads above his head. Sir Galahad remains on the station, tipping his hat to every woman who shares the platform space with him, until finally, if he wants to board the train, he has to jam himself as the 'last one in.'

And so in this way I calm myself after Doctor Trent's revelation that my ex-husband has invaded yet another part of my life.

My phone rings as I open the last lock and enter my apartment. I fumble to answer it, and notice an 8 by 11-inch paper on the floor that has been slipped under the door.

I bend to pick it up as I answer. "Hello?" Vincent sounds excited as he plunges ahead without a greeting. "You get my note?"

"I walked in the door this second." I am losing patience. "What do you want?"

"I asked you, you get my note?"

"I'm looking at it now." In a barely legible script, it informs me of Vincent's imminent arrival. *I'll be there at*

4:30. We've got a slot at the HNRG. I glance at the clock. It's 4:10. I haven't the slightest idea what HNRG refers to. I use my school teacher voice. "Vincent, what's this about?"

"If you don't know, I can't explain on the phone. I'll be there in a few minutes. Leave the apartment door open so I don't have to pick the lock." He ends the call.

I laugh and shrug. What can I lose? I have no other plans than to finish school work, and Monday is never a heavy load. It can wait. I start to remove my school clothes.

I am still in my undies when he blows into the living room. He takes one look into the bedroom and turns his back. "Geez, you always walk around like that? Don't tell me you wore that outfit to school today."

"Look all you want. I have to hang my school clothes in the closet, so enjoy the lingerie as long as you can." I am teasing him and he knows it. He turns toward me for a better view but by that time I have pulled on my jeans and am starting to ease a sweater over my head, but in no hurry.

"Okay, that's your game?" He comes without hesitation into the bedroom, snatches the sweater out of my grip, and licks both breasts, long, hot and slow. I feel I have been electrocuted. But he drops the sweater back in my hand and heads straight for the laundry room, where he removes the Ruger from the jewelry box where we've hidden it. He unloads it carefully and wraps it in newspaper. "Got a box?" I point to a shelf in the kitchen where I stack some paper bags and small flattened boxes. He measures one against the gun, then reconstructs the box, fits the Ruger into it, and seals it shut.

"Come on, let's move it. We have a slot at the range and can't waste time." He puts a gentle hand on my arm and leads me toward the door. "Bring your driver's license and any other ID you've got. These guys stick by the rules." He kisses the back of my neck as I lock the door behind us. "Most of the time, anyway."

16

The shop is on an untrafficked side street that backs up to a small strip mall around the corner, an oasis of commerce in a residential neighborhood. There's a sign on an awning above the window: "High Noon Rods and Guns." The span of windows is impressively clean, with a few signs that dictate all weapons to be checked at the door. Outside, an old man sweeps some fresh snow away from the door. There isn't much of it, but enough for a customer to lose footing. He tips his hat as we enter. I smile a nervous smile.

Inside, the shop is a large neat room bordered by showcases full of hand guns. The walls are hung with long guns, neatly stacked and arranged by size. It is quiet. "Right time of day," Vincent says. "Couple of guys already at it," he gestures to a closed door that leads to the property in the rear. I hear muffled explosions that I assumed are gun shots as we walk over to a long counter top where two men wait, looking us over as we approach. I do my own looking, at an older man with a thick beard and thicker glasses, and a youngish guy whose muscled arms are so covered in tattoos I mistake them for his shirt sleeves.

"Hey Vinny, how goes it?" The older man offers his hand and Vincent grasps it firmly.

"Good, Dino, making money and maybe making time." They both smile. The guy with the tattoos snickers. "Makin' time," he repeats. "That's awesome. My grandfather used to say that about hookin' up with his girlfriends. I didn't know you were that old," he addresses Vincent.

"Yeah, well, I have a good memory for the 20th century."

Vincent turns back to the older man with the thick beard, and starts a quiet conversation out of hearing range. I walk casually around the room, pretending I am not frightened by the weapons surrounding me.

The tattooed guy moves along with me as I explore, but stays behind the counter. "Ever shoot a gun before?" I shake my head, and lift a ladies' purse, a beautiful green leather clutch that has an empty holster in one compartment. He addresses me again as I put the purse back on its hook. "So were you ever in a gun store before?" I shake my head. I finger a shoulder holster tee shirt, padded at the neckline for comfort. "Ever load a gun?" I touch a long gun propped on a bipod, and read the label: Ruger 356 Takedown. "Hey, looka that. She touched one!" I try my best shut-up stare, the one I use in school.

He looks away, then over toward the two men talking. "Hey, she's a freaking virgin," he yells. "Never even killed nobody!"

The older man walks slowly toward him. His voice is low, intense, but audible. "Go out back into the range and pick up the used target sheets. And do me a favor, see if you can get yourself shot while you're out there."

Mister Tattoo walks sheepishly toward the back door, muttering about "people with no sense of humor." He closes the door harder than necessary as he disappears through it.

I walk back to Vincent as the older gentleman returns. "Young lady, we have a bit of a problem here. We don't allow anyone to use the range who doesn't have a permit. I was explaining to my friend here the rules we're obliged to obey."

I am relieved. Vincent puts his hand on the counter in front of the old gentleman, and brings me closer with his free arm so we are a threesome. "We get it, Dino, but like I told you, she needs to have a way to protect herself when she's alone. We want you to start the registration papers, but in the meantime, we have to do this now. We can't wait for permit papers to be processed, the class she'll have to take, the whole damn party. I just want her to know how to manage a handgun. It's the experience that she's missing. She already knows how to load and unload the chamber, but she needs a couple hours of practice. Her ex-husband has been stalking her, he even broke into her apartment and vandalized the place. We can't wait till the asshole does it again. And he hurt her, you know what I mean? Try to understand. If she was your daughter..."

Dino opens his hands in front of his chest and shrugs. "Yeah, you told me already. Vinny, this is New York City, not some dumb-shit town in Arizona, you know? What do you want me to do, lose my license?"

Vincent leans closer and lowers his voice. "It's not just about me, Dino. She's Frankie Petrillo's niece, and I can't go back to him with no for an answer, you know?"

Dino examines the countertop for a minute, nodding his head. "Yeah, Vinny, I hear you. I understand." He rubs his thick beard for a few seconds. He shrugs one shoulder. "Sometimes rules aren't good enough for a special situation." He looks up from the counter. "For Frank, I can do it."

"I won't forget this, Dino." Vincent extends his right hand.

Dino shakes it. "I know you won't." He rings a bell at the end of the counter. "Let's get the little lady started. Jimmy'll come in and get her in a minute, have her show him a few times how she handles the gun, and start her off." He smiles at me and pats my arm, hits a button on the shop phone. "Ready for a lesson? Don't be nervous, Jimmy's the best!"

Jimmy is wiry and solid at the same time, with red hair turning white and a smile meant to reassure. He reminds me, physically and in his actions, of my deceased father,

73

with his deliberate movements and careful actions. He and Dino have a short whispered conversation before he approaches us. Low key, quiet, he shakes hands with Vincent, and leads us toward the back of the shop. The three of us go through a double door into the range area, where an elderly couple is blasting away at the target with the speed and success that suggests frequent practice.

Jimmy addresses me for the first time. "Let's see your weapon, please." I turn toward Vincent, who is carefully removing the Ruger from the box. He hands it to me. I hold it without touching the trigger. My hand develops a tremor.

Jimmy doesn't miss my timidity. "We're in no hurry," he said. "Let me show you how to hold it." He guides my hand, fingers and all, into the right position. "How does that feel?"

I nod. "Okay, I guess."

"Good. Okay, put it down here on the rack. I'd like you to show me how you load it."

I look at Vincent. He has made me go through this process at least five times, loading and unloading, but at the moment I can't remember a thing. Both men look at each other over my head. Jimmy picks up a box that rests on the rack, and starts to open it. The label says 'Westminster.' There are numbers on it. 380 stands out in big letters.

I try to sound as if I know what's going on. "Three hundred and eighty bullets in that little box?" They both begin to laugh, and I join them. "Okay, okay, I never saw a box of bullets before," I acknowledge. Vincent gives me a shoulder hug, and Jimmy pats my arm. "These are three eighties," he says kindly, "the shell your weapon takes."

And so the lesson proceeds. Vincent takes a back seat, and remains quiet, but I sense his full attention. I have to load and unload the clip to Jimmy's satisfaction before he goes on to the next steps, which include holding the gun safely, racking a shell into the chamber, aiming at the target by looking down through its sights, and each step done about five times. The target is familiar, a piece of heavy duty paper, with a bullseye at the center, surrounded by ever-widening circles

"Now," he explains, "let me tell you a little about your weapon. It's good for range practice. It's a close range gun. It's up close and personal. Your weapon will make noise and can have a little kick," he explains. "The weapon tends to lift. Like this." He aims at the target and takes a stance, which he tells me to imitate. He insists I look again down the barrel before he takes the gun out of my grip and slowly pulls the trigger. The sound is not as loud as I expected. I've seen too many action movies. But the jolt after the shot is noticeable, as Jimmy's hand pulls up just a little from the level at which he held it.

I am ready to face my first real target. I assume the stance he has shown me. I hold the gun as I've been told, my left hand bracing my right as I steady the gun. My finger lies alongside the trigger housing, not to be on the trigger until I am ready to shoot.

I aim carefully down the barrel to the sight, put my finger on the trigger and squeeze. Nothing happens. I'm not squeezing hard enough. Jimmy rearranges my finger on the trigger to improve my leverage, and tells me to pull again. I aim again. This time I hear that satisfying click as the gun goes off.

The three of us check the target. I have managed to hit within the second circle. There are a series of high-fives and then Jimmy says, "Cool start. Now let's get down to business." I go through seven more targets before Jimmy agrees to let me stop. My shooting isn't bad, I sometimes shoot a tight group, but my successes are fewer as the practice session grows longer.

"She's beat," come the welcome words from Jimmy I've been waiting for. "Okay, call it a practice," he says. He smiles at me and then at Vincent. "She's beat. She did fine. Want to bring her back another couple of times, it's good with me. She's a good student and a pretty decent shot. Just see Dino for another appointment. He's the secretary and cashier, both." Vincent shakes Jimmy's hand and puts a Benjamin on the rack, ignoring Jimmy's objections. Dino won't take a cent. "No, really, Vinny. Pleasure to do Frank a favor," he says, and scribbles a date for our next visit on a card he hands to Vincent.

Back at the apartment, we feel celebratory. The snow has stopped, leaving only a few frozen flakes and a darkening day. The apartment feels cozy. Vincent sits on the couch, picking cashews out of the bowl of mixed nuts I've put in front of him. I bring him a bottle of Sam Adams and sit next to him, sipping my glass of sauvignon blanc. He tips the bottle toward my glass in a halfhearted toast. "So, you feeling safer?"

"I feel more...capable."

"Yeah, you got some good scores. But you know what I mean. Are you feeling like you could protect yourself if you had to?"

"You mean actually shoot somebody?" I take another sip from my glass and look down into it. "I don't think so."

He blows an exasperated sigh. "What do you think we went there for? It's not an amusement park, you know? It's a way to teach you to function alone if you have to. Deal with a stalker if you have to." He raises his voice. "Save your own damn life if the asshole shows up."

His anger scares me. I set my wine down and touch his shoulder. "I do feel a lot more independent, but maybe I'm just not ready." I look into those deep green eyes. "Maybe I can't picture waking up in the middle of the night and having to reach for that...*Ginger*. Or calling out 'who's there?' That comes across as just a horrible movie scene. And I'm not a good actor. Can you understand that?"

He stands abruptly, looking down at me. "What you don't understand is the guy's a psycho. From what you tell me, he's not giving up. Yes, damn it, you have to keep the Ruger handy and use it, close up, if he shows." He paces a few yards and looks out the window at the remaining crushed holiday decorations, melting their colors into what is left of the snow.

When he walks back to the couch, he bends down, moves my glass from my hand to the side table and raises me from my seat. He pulls me into the curve of one arm. I can feel his pulse against my wrist and I breathe the earthy scent of his underarm. He holds me in silence for what seems like a long minute. Then with his other hand, he gently plays with my hair. He moves his hand down my body under my sweater and begins to caress my breast. His gentle touch feels like a butterfly wing. I melt like a burning candle. I feel myself getting wet. I raise my head and graze his lips with mine.

"Damn. I *knew* you wouldn't be wearing a bra," he says. I am immediately furious. He's congratulating himself! How dare he touch me for the sake of exploring my lingerie? I start to pull away, but he circles my nipples one more time, draws a breath, and exhales an indistinct sound. It might be a laugh, but I'm not sure. "I hardly know how to keep my hands off you," he says. He takes a step back and puts both hands on my cheeks. "But I'm learning to do it."

He grabs his jacket from the back of a chair and heads for the door, buttoning the jacket as he goes. "Our next appointment at High Noon is Thursday after next. I'll pick you up around 4:00." He stops in the doorway and turns back to me. "Look, I'm sorry. I couldn't help myself. I swear, I didn't do that for fun."

I listen to him jump the last steps and close the downstairs door. I double lock my door. "Bastard," I whisper. I wonder for a moment what he meant by 'fun.' I decide he is a tease, plain and simple.

I need to vent. I won't tell Erin everything, but I promise myself I'll call her tonight. Now I sit at the roll top desk and start to review the pages of work I collected from 'my girls,' reminding myself that their straightforwardness is what I most love about them.

17

The Pour Room on Boylston Street is jammed. The din at 10:30 prevents any civil conversation, but Erin and I are having a good time just watching the crowd at the semicircular bar, and feeling old in a superior kind of way.

It has taken a little coaxing to get her to go, but I need the nostalgia. "A bar?" She looks at me as if I've suggested an opium den. "We always got our drinks for free! Why would you want to go to a bar?"

It takes a reminder of our advanced age and lack of Boston contacts to make her admit we probably aren't going to get any free drinks. My first gulp of my IPA justifies the decision. I am happy to be back in Boston for the weekend in her company, where we can remind ourselves of The Treetop, the best and only bar near Loreto, the small private college we'd attended in upstate New York.

She pokes me with her elbow. "Three o'clock on the circle," she says. I glance over from our stools, positioned at about six thirty. Whoever he is, he's definitely worth a look. Nice three-quarter profile, messy blond curls. Some long sleeved sport shirt, covered with print I can't read. Soccer? Football? I can't make it out, but he looks athletic. He's engaged in a conversation with an older man, but turns often in our direction.

"But he's only about nineteen," Erin adds, after a closer look. "Probably still letting his mother pick his clothes."

"That would be because he can't afford them himself," I say. "Maybe that's his dad."

"Looks like a coach to me. Or – please tell me this is

bullshit! – he's gay."

"Erin, please. I don't care if he is, he's great artwork. I could watch him all night."

"Yeah, well, he's watching us. If he ditches the guy he's with, I bet he'll come over."

It's just a half hour and two beers later that he does. I watch him walk his companion in our direction. He walks past us to the carved wooden door, where they exchange a hand shake. He turns back and stops at our stools. "Going out tonight, ladies?"

I stare at him. "That's what they ask prostitutes," I say.

He's immediately flustered. He opens his hands to show innocence, and tries to apologize. "Not what I meant. Really." He runs a hand through his curls, giving each of us a half smile. "I was just asking about your plans, maybe we can hit a party my friend's having up the street. Cool people, good drinks." He smiles at Erin. "Blondes especially appreciated." And to me, "No offense intended."

We're quiet, each of us waiting for the other to speak. His eyes focus on Erin. "My friend thought you looked like tourists, but I think I used to see you around, when I had a summer job here," he says. "Name's Matt. Matt Corey."

Erin points her index finger in his direction and squints, watches him a long five seconds. She moves her finger to her lips. "I think I remember you. But you're too young to have been behind the bar..."

He shrugs. "I was a bus boy." He smiles an angelic smile. "I was almost about seventeen. Not even old enough to drink." He looks away from us, embarrassed. "You guys were probably twenty, twenty-one... "I mean, I know you were still in school then, but now..." He trails off.

Erin raises an eyebrow. "Now we're senior citizens, is that it? Do we get discounts?"

"C'mon, you know I'm blowing it here. So you're older than me, so what. Come to the party. You'll have a good time, I promise." He hesitates. "I've gotta go. Told my friend Seppi I'd help with the snacks."

We ask him to write the address on a napkin, and wait till he's out the door. "What do you think?" we blurt the words simultaneously to one another. Erin replies first. "What can we lose? I'm not afraid." She gestures to the occupied stools. "Two dozen people saw him talking to us. He'd have some trouble explaining if something happened."

"So you want to go? It's almost midnight."

"We'll sleep good tonight," she says. "Besides, I'm starving, and the pub menu's not cheap. Besides, he likes blondes."

We slide off our stools and head for the door.

Rain begins to fall just as we find the address Matt has given us. The exterior of the town house is well kept, the wooden door impressively carved and warmly unlocked, but once the door closes behind us, we are in total darkness.

"You want to bail?" Erin grabs my jacket sleeve. "C'mon, let's go. It's creepy here."

"Maybe a bulb blew. You're the one who pushed for this. Let's see what's upstairs." I start my way up, holding on to the banister for security. Erin follows me, muttering curses under her breath. "If this turns out to be one of your damn disasters —"

She stops, pointing to a pool of light that spills out under the door at the end of the hall. We hear muffled music and a shriek backed up by laughter. Just as I raise my fist to knock, the door begins to open and a young woman crashes through it, blind to us as the music's intensity propels her down the stairs and out the front door.

No one comes to the open door. Now there is no light. We see shadows, but can't identify them, and no one even looks in our direction. It feels natural to step inside, despite the dark. Its shadows reveal a poorly maintained apartment, few pieces of furniture, a dimmed lamp and what might be a bar. We hear more screaming and laughter but still fail to see who's creating it. The music is like an outgoing tide, an undertow pulling us deeper into the room.

Something is going on in the corner, where a dozen or more people are jammed together at a bar. As my eyes get accustomed to the dark, I watch a young girl toss the contents of her glass down her throat, gagging as she does so. A second girl, young as the first, grabs the glass offered to her by the bartender and does the same. Neither of them can be fourteen, if I can trust my eyes and my familiarity with young women.

A third drinker swallows her drink with ease. "I got the good stuff," she crows. "That was some tasty shit. What's in it, anyhow?"

There's much laughter. "Who's gonna tell her?" someone shouts. Again, there is laughter and some shrieking. She is starting to look alarmed. Within a minute, a good looking frat boy comes over and puts his arm around her. She looks grateful for this attention. It gives her a sense of belonging. They head toward a closed door on the other side of the room.

Another young man escorts the remaining two drinkers past us to the door. Their walk is unsteady. "You gals go home now," I hear him whisper. "We'll let you all come back some other night and try again, but only if you don't tell nobody." They resist but his hold on them is firm. "Out," he says with definition, and closes the door as they throw a few four-letter words behind them.

I am not sure what we've just seen. Matt appears next to us suddenly, all smiles, and touches the back of Erin's head, smoothing her short cut blonde curls, as he explains. "It's our monthly contest, you might say. That's when we get the young ones initiated." He watches our faces. "But now their routine's done and the party goes on."

I shudder at the word 'initiated.' "Am I supposed to be

reassured?" I ask. "You say the party goes on. What happened here?"

"It's pretty harmless. You know, all these kids want to grow up fast. But they're also afraid their parents'll find out they've done something naughty. These are prep school kids, you know? We run into them hanging out near their schools. Some of them are on a tight leash, they're seventh, eighth graders maybe. But they have money. So they peel off a few bills, maybe more than a few, to us – me and Seppi – and for that, we promise to educate them and give them, um, an adult experience. Afterwards, they never know where they've been or who we are. We do it in a different house every month."

I can barely put words together. Erin is also mute, but I am finally unable to be silent. "Seventh graders? What the fuck are you talking about? You help 13-year-olds have sex?"

"It's not exactly like that. We make it a lottery, for fun. We pick three girls who swear they're virgins. We actually inspect them for that. The three girls have to drink. Two get whatever alcoholic drink they want, but with something disgusting in it, like cod liver oil, or worse. But they don't know ahead of time what they're getting, and they have to drink it all. Sometimes they get two chances, still with something lousy in it, but that's just to get them buzzed, you know?"

"Okay, I'm getting a picture of a completely illegal thing you call a game. What happens to the third girl?"

"Oh, she's the winner. She's gonna have sex with a handsome guy who's older than she is, and she is told ahead of time she won't remember any of it, but she'll know she's been fucked for the first time."

Erin finally breaks into the conversation. "How will she know?"

I stare at her. She hasn't caught on yet.

83

Matt gestures with his hands, opening them in a typical shrug. "It's obvious," he says. "She might remember the foreplay, she's sore in the right place, she's got some blood on her panties, we tell her she was terrific, she's half-awake by the time we drive her home in a limo and she sneaks in her house."

Erin again. "So why doesn't she remember?"

I grab her wrist and begin to pull her away from Matt. "Erin, she won't because the drink was a rufi. And she won't remember who screwed her, or where." I can't imagine continuing the conversation. I feel as if we've all had too much to drink. "Let's get the hell out of here."

Matt interrupts with a hand on my arm. "Oh, wait a second. Take it easy. Seppi said he wants to meet you. Or tell you something. Whatever." He gestured toward the older man we saw earlier in The Pour, who is walking toward us, looking at me.

We are already halfway out the door. Still furious, I am ready to spit in his direction, but he approaches with a hand held out. He has a strong handshake, and a way of freezing a person in place when he talks. "Nice to meet you in person," he says. "Heard a lot about you from your uncle."

I am dumbfounded. "You know my uncle?" I check on Erin, who is enjoying letting Matt kiss her neck and her hair.

"Sure, for years. Knew each other as kids. We're still in touch," Seppi says. "I haven't always been in Boston, you know? Back in the day, Frank and I – but you don't want to know my history. Name was Giuseppe then." He smiles, his laser gaze holding me.

I wait quietly for the next part of the conversation. Why is he talking to me at all?

"So Frank called me a day ago. He was trying to reach you at your home. Something about your locksmith, or your door lock. I didn't quite get it. But anyway, he emailed me a recent photo, which is why I recognized you when you were still at The Pour."

"You're not the only one who doesn't quite get it," I say. "How would he know I'd be here in Boston?"

"Let's both admit it, he keeps track of you. He knows she-" He glances over at Erin, still preoccupied with Matt. "Let's say he knows where she lives, and he knows you hang out together sometimes. He told me where I could find you if I had to." He stops, embarrassed by the expanse of his knowledge. "But I told him I was working, and then I saw you at the bar, so I never had to contact you, 'cause I had Matt invite you both here."

"Yeah, very comforting. Some stranger didn't come to Erin's door, looking for me. Shit, that would've scared me right back to Brooklyn."

"Look, I'm sorry to spring it on you, I don't want to get you upset. But do me a favor. Give him a call, tell him I spoke to you, tell him you're okay, and find out about the door lock or whatever he was in a twist about. He gets a little nervous about you, I think; you know, he feels like he's your guardian or something..."

He waits for me to speak but I can't get anything out of my mouth or my mind. "One more thing," he says. He stares past my eyes into my mind. "What you saw back there?" He uses his thumb to point to the party room. "That's got to stay there, you know what I mean? It's become a big deal for me and Matt, and so far we haven't had any issues, either with the kids or the cops. I know your uncle would understand that I'm asking you to bury it, capeesh?"

I can't swallow the words that fly out of my mouth. "Those are twelve-and-thirteen-year-old girls. You arrange parties where these kids- *kids!* – lose their cherries to some guy they'll never recognize again. It's disgusting!"

"Easy, go easy," Seppi says. "We make sure they're safe. The guys wear protection, they're careful. This isn't a rape, it's an introduction to adulthood, something the kids *want*. Your uncle would see it as a safe way to make a good living...and he'd totally agree with my asking you to keep it quiet."

I am done and I know it. Criminals know their way. And childhood friends like Seppi and Uncle Frank tend to stick together. The thought that Uncle Frank would condone sex parties for children is revolting. But I can't go against the uncle who has protected me for so long, who in spite of my need to escape his power, is responsible for saving my life at a time when I was most vulnerable. Besides, I fear him.

I feel the hatred filling my breath and thoughts. I pull away from Seppi's hypnotizing gaze. "Thanks. For the lesson."

I make my way to Erin, who is enjoying Matt's massage of her blond hair. "Train's leaving the station. Exchange phone numbers with your friend and let's go." She comes reluctantly toward me. "Do we have to go?"

I spit her name. "*Erin.*" She hears the tone rather than the word and steps quickly back to share some words with Matt. Hesitant, she joins me again. I hold her by the elbow and lead her down the stairs and out through the beautifully carved wooden front door.

18

Out on the street, we avoid the water that has collected in the last dark minutes. With little chance for conversation, we skirt the worst puddles, jumping from one wet cement slab to another. "As usual, no umbrella," Erin whines. "Could be worse, I guess." She flips her volume to a low mutter as she realizes I am not responding.

We reach the T and go down into the station, joining the crowds of late night party goers who are now going home or to the next party at someone else's apartment. "Smells like a wet dog down here, huh?" Erin shakes her blond curls and brushes water from her skirt, finally facing me with a relieved smile that quickly becomes concern.

"Kit! Why on earth are you crying?" She checks my wet clothes and glances at my shoes. "Did you hurt yourself while we were skipping those waterfalls? Did you sprain something?" Tears almost invisible on my already wet face, I look away from her. She puts her hand on my arm. "Is it about those young girls? I know that sucked, but we can't do anything about them now."

"Erin, it's my uncle." I stop to wipe my eyes. "All that other stuff was bad enough, but my uncle ..." I fish in my pocket for a tissue, with no luck. I use my wet sleeve to dry my face. "How do I deal with him? He knows where I am, all the time! He has spies everywhere who watch me. I can't stand it."

"He's just trying to protect you," she tries to soothe me. "With all the scary shit you told me, you should be glad someone's got an eye on you."

I sob as I struggle to speak. "You don't understand. It's not that he cares. He refuses to believe some of those things I told you, and yet he's still taking over my life. I have to cut myself loose somehow, but how?"

She locates a tissue in her purse. "Here." She pushes it into my hand. "I'm sorry, but I don't know how you can blow off the efforts of a man who saved your life."

The train rattles to a stop and we add ourselves to the damp crew that has pushed its way in. Standing next to a slick pole, holding on for balance, with Erin as close to me as the mob allows, I draw a few gulps of the musty air. "How would you like to be 26 years old and stalked by your uncle?" I hear the shrillness in my voice, and bring the volume down. "That's what it feels like. Seppi told me he *knows* where I am, no matter where I go. I feel like someone buried a GPS in my veins."

Erin seems exhausted, but she addresses my rant. "What can you do…" It is more a statement than a question. "Talk to him. Is there any way you can bargain with him, or scare him?" She lowers her voice. "There must be something you could threaten him with. All those family secrets…"

I laugh aloud. "Brilliant. But there's got to be a way to escape without having the FBI chasing him." I hug her. The train pulls into our station. We make our way to the exit and out to the street.

19

"Yeah, Mary, we had a helluva time! That Domenica, she makes me feel like a kid again." Uncle Frank waves in my direction. "Like her, all curves and no wrinkles!" It's just the three of us in Aunt Mary's kitchen. It started with my need to drop by one Saturday, hoping to beg my aunt for advice, but my uncle showed up, recently returned from still another glamorous trip with his mistress.

Aunt Mary smiles benignly. "Was it one of the Islands again?"

"No, no effing way. This time it was Paris. And let me tell you, Paris in the springtime? Unbelievable! Makes you want to you-know-what all day." He laughs, pleased with himself.

"Well, Frank, you're both lucky enough not to have the kind of work that chains you to a schedule. I'm happy for you and Dee. She keeps you young and healthy, looks like."

My aunt's comment about schedules is correct. My uncle's "work" requires his attention, but not necessarily his presence. And Domenica has been complaining to me for years that she's the bird in a gilded cage, waiting for him to tell her when they can fly off together, whether to a night club, a casino, a theatre, or the Virgin Islands.

My aunt puts a bowl of soup in front of each of us. "Nothing like Pasta Faggioli for lunch. Dense, but not too heavy. Eat." We sit quietly at the antique dining room table, welcoming the fragrance as well as the taste of my aunt's cooking. My uncle still has a smile on his face.

He wipes his bowl clean with a thick slice of Italian bread before he speaks. "You doing okay? School's good?" When I don't answer promptly, he pushes his empty bowl back and faces me, examining me as if I were a painting in a museum. "You look great. Beautiful as ever and looking in charge of the entire planet."

I spit a little of my soup back in the bowl and use a napkin to wipe my mouth. I make eye contact. "No, Uncle Frank. No way I *can* be in charge when you have me spied on every place I go." The words jump from my mouth like frogs. I haven't planned to address the issue in such a straightforward way.

"Ah, don't give me agita. How the hell else can I keep you safe if I don't know where you are?" He turns to check in with his sister. "Right, Mary? This one –" He slaps his hand on the table – "she thinks she knows what she's doing. She comes to me with crazy stories about break-ins and broken locks and me spying on her. It's the kind of bullshit – excuse me, Mary – a teenager dreams up."

My aunt moves her chair closer to me and reaches to hold my hand. "Sweetheart," she says, "your uncle means the best for you. I don't know what the issues are, but if you needed help, he'd turn the world upside down to make sure you'd get it. You know that. That's an unspoken rule in our family. We come to each other's rescue. But I thought things were going well for you. Good job, safe apartment, good friends..."

What can I tell her? How do I explain Seppi and the changed keys to my apartment and all the rest of it, including Joseph's multiple invasions of all kinds into my life, and my uncle's apparent unwillingness to fix any of the problems I've brought before him.

"I know you both watch out for me. But if you don't believe what I tell you, you're breaking the family rule of trust and confidence." This is blasphemy and I know it. But it's time to say what's on my mind.

My uncle gets up from the table. "I have to think about this. Kitty, maybe we've got to have a family conference. Sure, that could be a waste of time, but you seem to be unhappy with the status quo. I'll give it some thought, and let you know."

He kisses his sister on the cheek. "Mary, thanks for the lunch. I'll keep you in the loop. Don't let it bother you that she's acting immature. It'll all work out."

He lets himself out. I retrieve my jacket from the hall closet and try to soothe my unsettled aunt as she blots the tears on her cheeks. In this family, a conference is a big deal, meant to settle issues about money, crime and death.

"It's okay," I say, swallowing my fury. "It'll all work out. I've heard his family conference routine before. Not to worry, he won't follow through." I pat her arm gently. "After all, we're family."

She blows her nose, still obviously distressed. "I know. We both know." She accompanies me to the door and kisses me. "Take care." She's still at the door when I look back from halfway down the street. I wave and she throws me a kiss.

20

I sit at the back of the classroom with Becca, Noreen and Marta, a calendar opened in front of us. Lunchtime is over, and we're planning our Spring Celebration, which in reality is a pot luck lunch party that we started a couple of years ago. The idea came up one afternoon while we were discussing the value of wholesome food. Someone complained about the school lunch, and the discussion ended with every student naming a favorite lunch food.

With much lip-smacking, fake gagging and giggling, they had agreed that on one special late spring day, each girl could bring from home her own version of an acceptable lunch. We agreed on a cost limit. There would be no take-out restaurant food, and the rule was that no lunch was to be made by an adult. Becca now reminds us that it's her turn to bring dessert.

"I saw this recipe for the best cinnamon cookies. Crispy and spicy. I know I can make them." She looks at me. "And they don't have all sugar, neither... I mean, either."

"When do I get the dessert turn?" Marta jumps right on it. "Didn't ever do it, not once."

"That's 'cause you make the best mac and cheese," Becca says. "Everybody does her best thing, right Ms. G?"

Noreen, timid as usual, quietly chimes in. "And besides, Marta says she doesn't like dessert. 'Cause she's watching her weight."

Marta puts on her grownup face. "Not ever. Watching yours, probably." Noreen shrugs right back into her shell.

"Well, let's look back at last year's party list and see who

93

did what," I suggest. "And don't forget, by next year you'll probably all be in Mrs. Jeffrey's class, so no guarantee the Spring Celebration will work the same way...Marta, would you get those lists in the bottom drawer, left side, please?"

We're enjoying the quiet of a nearly empty classroom. With Doctor Trent at a conference in Albany, the mood is lighter than usual. In her presence, the young women acknowledge the respect she deserves, but her absence always creates an ease with them not often seen. They are growing up.

The nine cheerleaders have been called out to an organization meeting, and the four students who receive extra math help every other day are next door with their tutor. The three girls and I are comfortably relaxed.

I put two-year-old calendar lists in front of them. "Okay, think organization," I say. "Figure out whose lunches were main courses, whose were desserts. And who did duplicates of the year before. Then we can go from there. We have a couple of weeks yet, but don't drag your feet."

They put their heads together and start taking notes. Noreen, not a math fan, pushes herself away from the table. "It doesn't make no - I mean any - difference. It's a whole year ago. We can vote hands or do a lottery when the others come back, and that's that." She stands in her pool of apprehension, waiting for criticism. There is none, just a couple of nods. She beams.

At that moment, the four math students make a sudden quiet entrance. They show me the work they've done with the tutor and start to finish the task she's left them with. We are interrupted by the cheerleaders out in the hall, a signal that the day is approaching its last session. One or two are still repeating their lines. A scramble of laughter and conversation pushes the nine of them through the door, with the final appearance of Corina, yelling "last one in."

She makes her entrée as only Corina can, all smiles and sweeping arms. "And here he is, Ms. G. Last one in, and he says he's your boyfriend."

I stand up from the table. This can't be happening.

Joseph comes around the corner into the room, all slick, smiling and looking fabulous. He wears a dark blue suit, striped white and black tie, newly polished cordovans. He walks straight to me, enfolds me in a huge hug, and kisses me on the lips.

I can hear gasps and murmurs from the audience. I pull away, but I can't react. There are too many options. The alarm button under my desk is out of my grasp. I fear frightening my girls at the same time I fear for their safety.

He leans over Marta, Becca and Noreen, who are sitting frozen at the table. "Where'd all these beautiful young women come from?" he says. "I see women like this when I'm watching movie stars." They blush as only seventh graders can, trying not to giggle.

He turns his attention back to me and the others, holding me close. "Aren't you going to introduce me to your crew here?"

"How did you get into the building?" I hiss.

"Easy." He whispers. "Knew the Director was away for the day, got myself a visitor's pass at the desk." He waves a piece of paper at me and the girls. "So, when you going to introduce me?" he smiles that mask of charm.

"This is an old friend," I stumble into my explanation. "Not my boyfriend," I manage, "so you can't believe everything - or anything - he says."

He pretends shock. "Can you believe she said that? Just shows you can't trust women." He pushes me against the back wall of the classroom. "See what I mean? She'll probably pretend not to like this, either." He pats my buttocks and then begins to rub them, holding me firmly in a position that I cannot escape. The girls are dumbfounded.

I struggle out of his grip and try to hide my rage. "He's a terrible tease, never knows how to behave," I say, "and he's leaving right now, before we call the police to report someone is trespassing."

There are some low-key supportive "uh-huhs" and a few "yes, Ms. G." as they begin to sense my discomfort. Janina raises a tentative hand. "Want me to go to the desk? I can tell Miss French to call them."

Joseph moves toward the door. "Now, pretty girl, no need for that. I'm a peaceful man and I can see Ms. Gabrielli is pretending not to be a fan of mine. Well, I'll find another way to remind her that she belongs to me." He throws them all a kiss and escapes into the hallway.

"Ms. G., should I report to Miss French?" Janina asks again, unsure of her orders.

"Thank you, Janina. I'll take care of it. I'd like you all to get back to business and work with your groups. Use your graphing calculators." I walk slowly toward the Spring Celebration committee. "You three, finish your tentative lunch assignments and we'll vote on them tomorrow. Then join your graph groups. I'm right here if you need help."

I close the classroom door and circulate among the unusually quiet groups. I am in no condition to be useful. I decide to choose another day to clarify what has just happened. My sole intention is to keep them safe without suggesting that they needed protection. Besides, I do not want to face the life I am apparently still living, as the weak victim of a bully. The bell finally rings, accompanied by the scratching of chair legs and stacking of books. Ready to leave, they watch me, waiting for permission they don't need.

I search for the words that will send them out in comfort. "You were all very polite to our unwanted visitor," I say. "He did not belong here. It was a strange situation, and you handled it like adults. I can't explain all that happened, mostly because I'm not sure I know it myself. But I can assure you it will not happen again."

I surveyed the room. "Do you understand?"

Corina raises her hand. "Was I wrong to let him in?" she asks. "He said he was your boyfriend."

"Nothing to be guilty about," I say, feeling her discomfort. "You believed a grownup in a safe environment. It's not as if you met him in the street and invited him to come and meet your teacher." There are a few giggles. "And after all, Corina," I deliver as genuine a smile as I can summon, "you did your job and let the last one in." The quiet turns into babble as they respond to their familiar game and are reassured that no harm has been done.

I walk them down the hall to the main exit. They chatter among themselves and I know they'll have a story to tell when they see someone, anyone, at home. I wave at the last small bunch as they split into separate ways at the corner.

I straighten my back, align my shoulders and step back into the building to speak with Miss French. "Who was that hunk?" she asks.

"I'll tell you sometime when I write my memoirs," I reply, and give her as little information as I can about why she cannot ever give him a visitor's pass again, and why it would be wiser to call the police instead. She takes detailed notes.

21

On the way home, I stop at Family Court. A two-hour wait reveals that I can indeed restore the order of protection I have registered with the court in the past. I have not thought about it in more than a year. Nor have I realized it would expire.

The clerk is an older woman, beautifully dressed and properly dignified. Rows of dread locks add to her style. "Honey," she says, after I explain a skeleton version of my situation, "Why didn't you file the first time he showed up again in your life?"

She doesn't wait for a reply. "Thought you'd deal with it yourself, I bet, or figured your family would help you out. Not always a good bet, huh? Well, what happened is, the justice marked it 'expired' after one year. You just have to get a court date and ask that the OoP is restored."

She hands me a form to fill out. "Do it now," she advises. "I'll file it today and you'll hear back about the date. And watch your back in the meantime. You have to protect yourself. These slick characters think they have every right to get what they want." She sees my expression and laughs a quiet chuckle. "I got it right, didn't I?"

"Yes, Ma'am," I smile at her wisdom.

I walk away thinking of her advice that I protect myself. It has been some weeks since the last time I practiced at High Noon Rod and Gun. After several satisfying sessions, I feel secure and confident, but when Vincent announced his plan to be away for "a couple of weeks, maybe more," I lost any interest in practicing alone.

I think of the last time we were together, when he told me he was leaving. I run the memory of his visit like a bad movie. He is reluctant to leave the apartment. He follows me like a puppy, into the kitchen when I get him a beer, into the bathroom when I wash my hands, and into the bedroom when I change my shirt.

I am determined to stay out of his reach, unable to get out of my mind the way he has left me before, hungry for him and humiliated by his ability to arouse me. We sit for a few moments in the living room, when he suddenly gets up and walks over to the front window. He looks up and down the street, scratches his jaw, takes a piece of gum from his jeans pocket. He removes the wrapper and puts the gum in his mouth. He looks up and down the street again.

He is making me nervous. "What is it? What are you looking for?"

"Nothing. Really. Just thinking."

"Thinking what? You have something to tell me?"

He looks suddenly relieved. "Yeah. Yeah, something like that."

"Spit it out. What's up?"

"I feel bad to tell you. I have to go away for a while."

Shit, I think, he's going to jail. "Tell me what's going on. What did you do?"

He crosses the room, and joins me on the couch. "I didn't do anything. Jeez, I don't get the way you are. What are you thinking?"

This is getting ridiculous. "Okay, I'm not asking any more questions. Just say what you've got to say." I move away from him on the couch.

He moves closer. He cups my face in his hands. He delivers one of those kisses that shuts the rest of the world out. He finally moves his lips from mine. "You don't know how it feels," he says.

"Of course I do. You just sucked the soul out of my body.

That's how it feels."

"Well yeah, but that's not what I mean. I have to tell you I have to go away, and I don't want to."

"Don't want to tell me, or don't want to go?"

"Yeah, both. See, Frank's sending me to Quebec for I don't know how long. I *can't* say 'No, I don't want to leave your niece.' But I don't want to leave you. You understand?" He moves even closer.

"Why Quebec?"

He shows me an embarrassed smile. "I speak a little French. Don't know if I'll need it, but just in case. You know your uncle, covering all the bases."

I don't ask any questions about his familiarity with French. He probably has dozens of other secrets I'm not aware of. "How long will you be gone?"

"That's the problem. Maybe a couple of weeks, maybe a couple of months. You can't call me. I can't call you. No contact with anyone but your uncle. Can't text, no email. My phone's going to be bugged, I don't know why."

"Ever hear of a disposable phone?"

"Sure. But I don't know who's going to be watching me, tailing me, eavesdropping. Last thing I need is to have your uncle mistrust me. But whatever, it's going to feel like I left my skin with you." He moves in for the closeup, picks me up and heads for the bedroom.

"This is not happening," I spit. I pull out of his grip and stand in front of him. "You've already fucked up my life and made me a gun-toting crazy woman. And teased me like a puppy with a bone." I know it makes no sense but I can't stop. "Kissed me, touched me in all the right – or wrong - places. Left me wet and wondering."

"I know, I know, and that's why I want to make it right. I can't keep you out of my head, I can't keep my hands off you. But your relationship with your uncle, he gets between you and everyone you know, the way I get it. He told me way back you were off limits, the day after I changed your locks and wanted you ten times more than I wanted the dinner you made me."

"Vincent." I don't know what to say next. "Vincent. You're very attractive and I've wanted you, too. But you don't know my uncle. If he said leave me alone, you could be in danger."

"The only pass I got was telling him about the range, and that you were learning to shoot. He thought that was a great idea, said you could use the practice, and he was even more okay with it when I told him Dino made an exception for you because of who you are. I mean, who *he* is."

Vincent holds me so tight I feel as if we are one person, but I can't figure out which of us is inside the other. "Oh," he adds, "I didn't tell him about the gun, I mean about Ginger; I wasn't sure he'd like that, you having a gun in the house."

"We have to be very careful," I say. "He's got a big ego, and expects to be obeyed. In everything, you know? He's got connections I don't even know about." There is a long pause. "It's good you're going away for a while. We both have a lot of thinking to do. Whether we want to risk anything. Whether we really want each other. Whether it's worth it."

"It's worth it to me. It's worth everything to me." He walks away from me and paces back. "I guess you're right. I'll go where he sends me, we'll let some time go by. If the job is a success, he'll be in good spirits. By the time I'm back, it could be summer. Maybe he'll soften up about me and you."

"Keep dreaming," I say, but I lean up for a kiss and close my eyes so I cannot see his face. "We'll find each other again. I promise. Be safe, be careful."

Our lips meet. When he pulls away, he kissed my eyes, my throat, my earlobes. "Be safe. And be mine," he says. He grabs his jacket and heads for the door.

Reliving that day, still remembering the woman at Family Court, I start to feel safer, and I hope that Vincent will return to me soon.

Alone in a world without Vincent, crazy scenarios become the norm, but they are all in my head. Now that Joseph has invaded nearly every corner of my world, I cannot stop wondering where he will appear next. Will it be at the supermarket? The dentist's office? The subway station? Aunt Mary's house? I look behind me everywhere I go.

What if I were to fly to Las Vegas? Would he even know I was there? For a moment I imagine it to be the perfect hideout. The remaining shreds of my sanity convince me it is *not* a good choice. The idea of sharing the same air with my uncle and my ex-husband is almost laughable. But too terrifying to make me laugh.

22

Of course Erin calls later in the day, in response to my voice mail. We have long ago agreed that texting and emailing are good for confirming meetings and cancelling plans. Real conversation requires a phone call.

She hears me out. "He showed up in your classroom?" She isn't an easy person to shock, but her voice reflects her incredulity. "You called the cops?"

"No, he bailed as soon as the word fell out of my mouth."

"So he got away with it..." She is quiet for a full minute. Finally she breaks her silence. "I can think of only one thing."

"Anything will help," I say. Just listening to her is therapeutic. Sometimes what she says is so funny it changes my whole view of the situation. I'm hoping for that kind of comment now.

"You need to leave town."

I laugh on schedule. Another one of her jokes. "I have a job, Erin. Remember?"

"Summer's around the corner, maybe around the block. It's May, you'll be done soon. Tell your Principal you need personal time. And then buy a one-way ticket to somewhere."

"No way! Georgia Trent needs me in June. Those last two weeks after exams, that's when the kids are most fidgety. "

"So let them fidget with a substitute."

"Erin!"

"No, don't 'Erin' me. Okay, so you stay for the exams, give them their grades or whatever other paperwork is required, and get a few days' leave. Wherever you choose to go, I'll take a week off, and spend the first week with you."

"Great suggestion, even though it reminds me of a fairytale. And you're the fairy godmother."

"Listen, I mean it, my plan is realistic."

"Realistic has nothing to do with it," I say, and gently end the call.

Something continues to appeal, even though I can't imagine running away. I need to think. She is my friend, sometimes serious, sometimes seriously nuts. I need to consider in which category her plan belongs before I offend her friendly willingness to help.

I lie awake nights thinking of Erin's idea. It seems so impossibly magical, like a romantic movie. But still, the script keeps running through my mind. After all, an escape doesn't have to be permanent. I can disappear for a short time, take advantage of my summer freedom.

Vincent invades my thoughts, but he's somewhere in Canada, and who knows where or for how long? Still, I fantasize. I can join him, I think. All I need to do is find him, and we can hide from all the people who make our lives crazy, my uncle included. We can rent a small apartment in Quebec. I will learn a little French, and get a job as a bilingual shop girl. We'll have wild, wonderful sex every morning and night, finally gratifying the longing we've been enduring for so long.

Tormenting and exciting as I find this, I know how impossible it is to accomplish. I resign myself to Vincent's inaccessibility, I know the trouble I might cause him. I wake up nights thinking of foreign places to visit, of ways to disappear and never be found. I have no idea where to go. But, I think, the world is large and there must be many options. Erin is right. I need to escape, if only for a while.

23

I'd like to think it's a coincidence that I literally bump into Cliff - or he into me -the next day. After class, I am delivering a fat manila envelope of test results to a gal I know in Greenwich Village, who's analyzing recent score results for middle schools in Manhattan. Mission accomplished, I am heading for the subway stairs when a hand touches my shoulder. But not just touches, it cups my shoulder in a familiar way.

I whirl. "What –"

Cliff stands there, a warm and friendly smile on his handsome face. He takes my hand and holds on to it. "Hey, what are you doing down here in the Village?"

"I could ask the same question, considering you work in mid-town." But I return his smile.

"Had to meet a friend at the New School, and decided to take a walk. Work off the debris of the day."

"I'm sure you work hard these days. How are your parents?" I'm so polite I can hardly stand myself.

"Still pillars of the Saratoga community, thanks, and hanging on to their reputations. Dad's still talking about retiring but I doubt he'll ever make the move. If he does, they'll move closer to me." He steps back and examines me with interest. "Looking great, Kit. You're still the same old girl you used to be, and that's pretty good."

I remove my hand from his gentle grip. "I remember that song, and as I recall, she wasn't a very nice old girl."

"I have some memories too, as a matter of fact, and the girl I'm thinking of did me wrong." He maintains eye contact.

We stand awkwardly, I with my guilt, he with the feelings he might still have for me.

"I really should go," I finally say. "You're messing with some history I almost forgot." I take a couple of steps sideways, ready to head for the subway.

"You mean *wanted* to forget."

He's in my way, blocking my path. I don't try to get past him. "I guess we know each other too well," I say.

"That's exactly what I was thinking." He puts his hand out and touches my forearm. "How do you feel about sharing a cup of coffee? Won't cost either one of us a thing," he gestures toward the coffee shop a few steps away. "I know the manager."

"Another one of your connections?"

"One of my clients at the bank," he says. Gently he steers us in the direction he has in mind.

I think of resisting, but abruptly aware of the heartless way in which I sabotaged our friendship, I submit.

The shop is built for shadows and light, the walls painted dark blue and the windows reflecting the afternoon sun. Corners are welcoming and secretive. The sign hangs above the bar: *The Silent Bean*. It's quiet at this time of day. No matter where we sit, we will not be within earshot of the few customers who sit, absorbed in their tablets and cell phones. Activity seems suspended, lingering between the lunchtime crowd and the wave of exhausted workers who will need a caffeine jolt at the end of a long day.

Cliff leads me to a secluded table in the corner. "This okay? We can sit nearer the window if you like. Or do take out and walk as we talk."

"I'm satisfied being off my feet for a change."

"Done," he says. We settle into the thin cushions on our wooden seats just as an attractively plump woman approaches us. She wears a silky wrap dress, a hot pink that highlights both her brown skin and her curves. She looks dressed for business, carrying her fifty or so years with dignity. She sports no apron, just a pleasantly alert expression. Cliff rises from his seat to greet her. "Sabina, this is Katherine, an old friend from college. Katherine, Sabina is one of my best clients, and a woman who understands how a business works."

Sabina gives me a welcoming grip. "Very nice to meet you. You're most welcome here, especially if *he* brought you." She smiles a crooked grin. "He gets privileges, you know."

Cliff pats her hand before he sits down again. I can see their mutual but neutral affection. I'm reminded again of his innate kindness, which got me through many unhappy days in the past. "First privilege," he says, "we'll have two iced mochas. We're having dessert before dinner," he adds, as she heads for the coffee bar.

He smiles as she walks away. "She is one of the most intelligent women I've ever worked with," he says. "She learns fast, and she gets the point, immediately. Sometimes she corrects me!"

"Well, your job's always been your focus. You're probably a good teacher, and you've obviously been a success. You always knew the next right thing to do." I smile at him with my eyes. "For example, how did you know I wanted a mocha?"

"Because I know you better than anyone I've ever met. And you know me better than anyone *you* ever met. You confided in me so many times," he says, reminding me of my former dependence on him. "You had so many secrets, but you made them *my* secrets as we got to know one another." He is quiet as the sweet drinks are delivered to the table. Sabina takes one look at us and bustles back to the bar. Clearly, a woman of discretion.

We sit there slurping our mochas for a few minutes. As

Cliff finishes his, he leans toward me. I squirm, not sure what's coming. "Kit," he says.

I head him off. "Cliff, I don't think I can handle a serious discussion right now."

He eases the tension with a tease. "What makes you think I'm serious?"

I have already thought it over and I'm ready. "Because you are. Because I screwed things up. Because I was incredibly unkind to you. And you didn't deserve it." I am surprising myself with my little speech, but it's what I feel needs to be said. "I want to clear the air," I say, pushing aside the dregs of my drink.

"It's been clear to me for a long time," he says. "It's simple: I protected you, we shared secrets, we fucked, you freaked. It couldn't get much clearer."

"I guess that's the short version. But we had been *friends*. I couldn't absorb that we'd suddenly become... whatever we suddenly were." The word 'lovers' is on my tongue, but I can't spit it out.

His voice remains low. "Yeah, I got that message, after a half dozen nasty phone rejections and another half dozen unanswered calls."

I am ashamed. He is right. I swallow hard. "Want to make friends and be nice? Like when little kids forgive each other?"

"Kit, we'll always be friends. We got through too much junk together to lose that. What matters is, do you think we can pull off being nice?"

I look down at the table, afraid to meet his gaze. I can speak now only in a whisper. "We can try..."

His expression hardens. "Fuck that. You don't understand the word 'try.' One mishandled moment of intimacy and you closed a door without trying." He rises from his chair and walks over to the corner of the bar, where Sabina is still doing paperwork. He drops a few bills on the bar. "See you 'round the block," he says to her.

"You too. Take care." She doesn't get up from her work.

Pausing for a moment, Cliff motions to me. "Come on, I'll walk you to the subway." He puts a determined hand under my elbow and leads me out to the sidewalk. At the corner, the subway entrances mark their destinations, uptown and downtown. "Which direction?" he says. "I don't know any more where you live."

"Back to Brooklyn," I reply. "I'm in the same apartment."

"Oh, so you see the scene of our crime every day, huh?" He's almost laughing, but he sees my discomfort. He puts one hand on my arm, sliding it partly under my jacket sleeve. "I know I'm being an asshole. I'm sorry."

We face each other, neither of us able to depart graciously. Finally, he gives me a three- quarter sideways hug. "No hard feelings, we both acted like babies." He kisses my cheek. "Okay if I give you a call one of these days?"

It would be way too awkward to refuse. I nod. "Sure. Number's the same."

"Why haven't you changed it?" he says.

I have never thought about it. "Good question. Guess I didn't want to lose all my friends." I wave and make my way down the cramped stairway without looking back.

The train is already in the station and starting to close the doors. I squeeze myself into the last car, and manage to get a seat in a crowded corner. I hope the rhythm of the train will soothe me, or at least hypnotize me, but I must be expecting too much. For the entire trip, the car rattles like a storm without lightning, and I cannot keep Cliff or our conversation out of my mind as it replays like a chorus in a cheesy song, all beat and no melody.

I call Erin as I exit the subway and start the walk down DeKalb Avenue toward my apartment. She reacts with interest to my report, but her reaction is harsh. "What bothers me, you slammed a decent guy like Cliff out of your life because of a romantic moment you weren't ready for, and you married a far-from-romantic bum who did the slamming in a totally different way, if you recall the black and blue marks." She rants for a few more minutes and insists I tell her she's correct. Which she is.

I try to defer her lecture. "What's up with Matt, your Boston baby?"

"Baby's the right word. Remember we said he looked young? Understatement of the year. Juvenile and dumb besides. I dumped him." She goes on, back to her question machine. "So, will you be friends with Cliff again if he calls? Or take it where he's always wanted it, a full blown sex-on-the-kitchen-table relationship?"

"Erin! Enough! Sometimes I wonder why I tell you anything. I don't have a plan. And I'm sure he hasn't got one either. And besides, he hasn't called yet, and maybe he never will. I told you, it was a very chaotic conversation. Both of us got pissed off at one time or another and by the time we separated we were like two strangers who struck up a pleasant but pointless conversation at a bus stop."

"Plenty of people meet at a bus stop and get married."

"Okay, okay. I'm just letting you know this relationship has nowhere to go at the moment."

"See? The magic words are 'at the moment'."

"Gotta go. I'll give you a call later."

"Later?"

"Yeah, like later this year!"

She laughs. "Kit, you rock. Check in with you soon."

24

My uncle is waiting for me on the steps of the brownstone. I'm starting to consider it an official waiting area. He rises as I turn from the sidewalk to the house. "My beautiful niece," he kisses my right cheek, ends with a grandma-type pinch for the left cheek. "Where've you been? I've been waiting an hour or more. Thought you'd be home from school by now."

"Had a couple of errands to run." I curl my free arm around his. "Nice to see you, Uncle Frank. Come on upstairs, I'll put the coffee on."

He follows me, breathing a little heavily as he climbs the steps. Inside, he seats himself on the couch, making use of the nearest comfortable seat. He runs his eyes over the brace lock with a certain satisfaction. "That Vinny, he knows what he's doing. That contraption," he gestures at the door, "couldn't be much safer if it was for a bank vault. Does good work, Vinny does. Any time you need something done, just let me know, I'll send him over."

"Yeah, he's a good guy," I say from the kitchen, adding the beans to the coffee grinder, relieved I don't have to look at him.

I smile as I place two coffee mugs on the small table in front of the couch, along with a handful of shortbread cookies. "So to what do I owe the honor of your visit?

He snatches one of the cookies, biting into it with total attention. "My favorites! These little scotty dogs knock me out." He holds up the remains of the now-deformed canine figure. "See? First I eat the head." He swallows two more

113

scotty dogs with gusto before I pour the coffee; he wipes the last crumbs from his moustache. "Not as good as cannoli, but I'm not complaining."

"Bet you behead chocolate Easter bunnies, too."

He produces that laugh, the one that sounds like a pit bull with a cough. I'm quiet, waiting for an answer to the question he has ignored.

He surveys the room, checking the roll top desk, the second hand rocking chair, the old but beautiful Oriental rug on the clean wooden planks. "Nice place. You did a lot with these things that your grandmother left, rest her soul, considering Bianca and Nina got first dibs after she died. Of course, you didn't have a place for anything then. No parents, no house of your own..." He is relishing his moment of nostalgia.

"You don't need to remind me that you and my aunts sold my parents' house after they were killed. And I was in college, not looking to be the Martha Stewart of my dorm. So I took the family leftovers when I rented this apartment. And it's good enough." I raise my open palm to encompass the sparsely furnished floor. "Anyway, it's safe now that Vinny's changed the locks, and that's what's important to me."

My uncle nods. "So you're okay now, right? No more break-ins, no more creeps invading your space. Secure as my jewelry case now that the problem is solved."

The idea that the problem is solved because he says so makes me furious. "Why are you even talking about this? When I told you I needed help, you blew me off. Told me I was imagining things. Said you couldn't help me, that Joseph was your number one and doing such a fabulous job, you couldn't believe he would break his deal with you."

Uncle Frank looks offended. "No, Kitty, you got it all wrong. It's true that Joseph's good at what he's doing. Sure, I have to keep an eye on him, but I trust him. He wouldn't dare break our deal. He learned early on you were off-limits, that his stint in Vegas was to keep him away from you. And your story that he broke into your place, that he held you here, was unbelievable. I always knew where he was, and it wasn't here. Kit, I've got my spies. What you thought wasn't possible!"

I can barely breathe. "You trust *him*? You don't believe me? You're the one who has your spies follow me wherever I am, who report back to you when I'm visiting Erin in Boston, you're the one who has connections in every corner of the world that I might venture into! You call it protection but it's control, plain and simple. You make me feel like I'm on probation. You believe your surveillance of Joseph is waterproof. Nothing more than ego on your part, because you refuse to be wrong!"

My uncle puts his coffee on the table. "Got a little cognac? I need a drop in my drink." He waits for me to find one of the few bottles of hard alcohol I have on hand. He adds a small pour to his cup and sips with satisfaction.

He shifts in his seat. "You're acting like a kid," he says. "Joseph has proven himself to be valuable and trustworthy. I am not going to dump him because you are hysterical over some imagined invasion. Or whatever you call it." He removes a cigarette from his shirt pocket, and rolls it to straighten it. I can tell he's getting ready to bail. He doesn't attempt to light the cigarette. He knows better.

"Think about that time and your story, Kitty. When you told me that stuff, maybe you were having a bad time. Maybe getting over the flu. Maybe caught some bug from those little girls you teach. Kids are always sharing germs. Next thing I heard from you, it sounded like you were having a breakdown."

He raises himself with some difficulty from the couch. I back away as he approaches me but I can't escape his embrace. "Please," he says. "You're my niece. I do my best to watch out for you. Don't let a few set-backs twist your view of the way our family does things. You don't need rules to know the family code."

I am emboldened by his mention of the rules. "Uncle Frank, all I care about now is that you leave me alone. I depended for years on your protection but now I've figured out how to protect myself." He still holds me loosely, patting my back as if I were an infant.

I close my eyes and picture Ginger, 'my friend the gun' that Vincent has insisted I learn to use. I ramble on, mocking my uncle's vision of me as one who needs his help. "I need to be on my own. I can do whatever it takes – check my locks every day, don't walk the streets, stay home when it's dark, carry my cell phone, use 911, carry a hatpin in my purse, don't talk to strangers –"

"Okay Kitty, I got the picture. You're not a child. But now you and I have to do what I think is best. And you have to accept my role in your life. Capisce?"

"Your role in my life?" I hear my volume increase as I gather my words. "Let's agree you keep *out* of my life. I'll call you if I need you. I remember a time when you tried to keep me safe. But since I've told you what you call a story, a story you refuse to believe, I haven't been able to count on you. Your so-called 'role' has been useless."

He releases me from his hug. "I see where you're coming from, your attitude. It's not going to help either one of us. You think you grew up? Probably don't even know what that means. We'll talk again. Soon."

He pushes past me to the door, turns the unlocked knob and leaves without closing the door. "Be careful," he calls as he makes his way downstairs.

I need a massage, or a bath, or whatever else a spa can provide. I settle for a nap.

25

When the phone rings late Saturday afternoon, the first name that comes to mind is 'Cliff.' I take a moment to add another drop of red wine to the couple of ounces I just poured. I want the wine to last through a comfortable conversation with my old friend, and I know in my heart I want it to be a long one.

I click on the call without allowing myself a glimpse of the caller ID. "Hi, happy Saturday," I start with.

"What are you doing right now?"

I know the voice, and put the phone down on the kitchen table. I don't even want to touch it, and I disconnect the call. It rings again. And keeps ringing. Finally, I turn the phone off. But I don't want to be cut off from the world. I may know *who* it is, but I don't know *where* he is. I turn the phone back on, my fingers controlling the slight tremor they've suddenly developed.

I ask myself why I haven't had the phone number changed long ago, and have to admit I have been waiting all these months for Cliff to call. Everything will have to change now, phone number for sure, but I'll have an excuse to contact him, and somehow Vincent, or neither of them will be able to find me. What is wrong with me, that I'm drawn to such different men, both of whom care for me? In my state of near-panic, there are no solutions.

It's no surprise when the phone rings again. "Funny," Joseph says, "the phone shut down and then came back. How do you think that happened?" As usual, he's mocking. When I don't reply, he continues. "So, what are you doing tonight?"

"Working, and I have no time to talk."

"You're not getting my message. I want to – need to – talk with you. In person."

"Not happening," I say, and disconnect again. I recollect my fears and turn the phone on again. Obviously, he's nearby, or wants me to think so. What if he tries to get in?

He texts. 'Normally I could get the locks open and just come up, but the key guy's away so I have to depend on your trust. Bum's not in town, just when I need him.'

When I don't reply, a notification from the phone reports another text. 'That key guy's usually a big help, but can't get to him right now,' he writes. 'Please let me come up. I just want to talk, I swear.'

I don't respond. My mind keeps going back to the "key guy," who's not in town. Is he talking about Vincent? Is that who originally got him into my home to damage my clothes and my piece of mind? I don't want to believe this about Vincent. There's more than one locksmith in Brooklyn, I think. I wish. But I can't be sure.

The phone rings again and Joseph's already talking. "You know, we didn't get to settle all the little things last time I was at your place. We never got a chance to glue our marriage together again."

Despite my memory of the "last time," when he forced himself into my apartment and I was repeatedly bullied and raped, I keep my voice calm. "Joseph, we are divorced. There's nothing to glue together. You have outrageously invaded my life, taken advantage of the situation I'm in... My uncle can cause you great trouble if I tell him all you've done."

He laughs. "Tell him what? Your uncle heard all your shit. And he didn't believe you. You know why? Because he trusts *me*. And he thinks of you as some young girl who imagines things that never happened and dramatizes things that did." He snickers, still complete amused by the role he plays with my uncle.

I can hear the smug smile in his voice and I hate him for it. My instinct is to disconnect but I need to know where he is at this moment. "Well, my uncle is in denial about my discussions with him. He doesn't accept that I'm an adult now. Anyway, I have to go. No time to talk."

"Aw, give me a break. I want to see you. I want to visit your pussy. It's in my mind all the time, Kit. Don't put me through this again. I need you."

I realize just how crazy he is, but I have to determine his location. "Sorry, I'm busy just now. Not possible to have company." My anxiety grows as I continue to wonder about the identity of the locksmith.

I'm stalling. "How did you get in the first time, when you wrecked my clothes?"

"Look, if you must know, I know people. There's a guy from the old neighborhood, knows how to pick locks. Nobody you know. Your uncle doesn't even know him. Danny could probably open doors without even touching them. Some people just have that talent, you know? Me, I could break the door down, but I'd still never know how to work the lock. So don't make me do something stupid, come and get me. Please. Kit, I'm out here on the street, it's probably going to rain any minute. I have to see you. Come down and let me in."

I feel some relief as I decide that Vincent was not instrumental in the break-in that started all this. "Look, I have an order of protection against you. You can't be within a hundred yards of me. If I even think you're in the neighborhood, I'm supposed to call the police."

"Damn, woman. Am I going to have to measure how far away I have to wait? Where I wait doesn't matter. You come out to go to the supermarket, I'm here. You go out for a walk, I'm here. I can wait as long as I have to. Your uncle won't be looking for me till Monday, so I can wait all day tomorrow and Sunday night, hot to have you up close to my body again."

I consider calling my uncle to ask about Joseph's schedule, but haven't I recently announced my independence? I clearly remember saying, less than a week ago, in a most definite voice, "Let's agree you keep out of my life."

It doesn't make sense to call the police, either. They'll ask exactly where he is, and I won't know. At best, they'll send a patrol car into the neighborhood, but without a clear picture of what to search for: a tall good-looking guy, bronze skin, likely to be well dressed. Plenty of those around.

I'll have to live with it, and hope I can outwait the psycho who claims to be waiting for me just outside my house. For now, I'm a prisoner in my own home. There's no way I'm stepping out into the street until I feel comfortable that he's gone. I calm myself, thinking of a lazy Saturday night and Sunday, looking ahead to a hot bath by candle light, a difficult night's sleep, and several hours of intense but absorbing school work.

It doesn't quite work out that way, as I find myself searching my mind all day Sunday for ways to get Joseph out of my life. An accident? A murder? A mistaken victim of a hit man? I fall asleep both nights with an image of Ginger-the-gun in my hand, my finger squeezing a friendly trigger.

Monday, I awaken early, still wrestling with my anger. I'm going to have to take Joseph's word about his whereabouts. Despite my fury and fear, I dress in my trim little summer suit, pack my school brief case and keep my phone at hand. Out on the street, all is quiet. Even the Spring saplings are quietly in motion, their new leaves tender and green. There's no one to be seen. I take a deep breath to control myself and head for the Lafayette station, already planning the start of my day. I whisper to myself, "I will find a way."

26

One evening the phone rings - yes, another phone call - and I check the ID. I don't recognize the caller, something like HNRG. It doesn't ring a bell. Still, I reply, and identify the voice that comes through. "Miss Gabrielli, it's Dino, from High Noon."

"Oh, Dino." I'm embarrassed as I try to think of the last time I was at the range. "I know you must be wondering what happened to me. I've been so busy with my job..."

"No worries, Miss. Wanted to tell you I ran into your uncle at a family meeting a few days ago, and he spent half the lunch break raving about you. Frank was excited that you've been coming to the range, and you know, grateful that we're helping you and all." He stops to breathe. "I'm calling to let you know how pleased he says he is, and I don't want him to think we don't follow up on our clients, you know?"

"Dino, I understand. You want him to think I'm so satisfied that I show up every morning between breakfast and lunch, and on my coffee breaks too, to improve my relationship with my gun." By the time I finish speaking, were both laughing. "I get it, Dino. I'll come by as soon as I can. It's just that Vincent's got a big assignment right now, and I feel uncomfortable showing up alone."

"Yeah, I heard about that. He's not back yet? Geez, bummer. Where the hell is he? Do we have to send the Italian National Guard to bring him back? You know, I got friends who probably could bring him back, if you got any info on the location."

"Beats me, Dino. I'm not on the "for-your-eyes-only" list. Don't know where, why, or how to reach him. But I promise, I'll show up at the range one of these afternoons and turn the target into a doily, okay?"

"Really, thank you Miss G, and I'll be sure to keep an eye on you so you don't feel alone. You know, I'll check on you and help out if you need me." I reassure him that he has been helpful enough, and he sends me a loud fatherly kiss over the phone. Dino is grateful that his shop will still be a magnet for Frank's niece.

That night, I keep reviewing what he said, that he 'has friends.' I wonder what else they can do, besides find people. Can they make them disappear? I begin to pursue the thought. I cannot help but recall an incident from the terrible days when Joseph and I were still together.

We were waiting for the train at the Ninth Street station. It was a quiet time, about one in the afternoon (not that the subway was ever quiet). The station was sparsely occupied. A few elderly women were carrying purses and hugging what looked like empty tote bags, meant perhaps for the shopping trip ahead.

Joseph had just delivered another of his ugly remarks, criticizing my looks, or my dress, or my intelligence; I can't remember the specifics. I can only remember that, as the train roared into the station, I had this wild notion to push him off the platform onto the tracks. No one, I thought, would see how it happened. The old women would be clueless. I enjoyed for a moment the imagined euphoria of his absence, and then it was over. The train slowed, Joseph grasped my upper arm with force, and when the doors opened, we entered and sat silently.

Yes, I remember wishing him dead. But I have never before considered the possibility of having him killed. Until now. I promise myself I'll find a way to raise the subject with Dino when I visit the range again. I shudder as I realize that I have not escaped very far from my uncle's grasp, or from his ways.

27

In the west, the sun is setting slowly, hanging some distance above the gentle hills below. It's a flaming orange-red, smeared with horizontal strips of light. We are sitting in a small plaza, where our cappuccino has just been served. It's pleasantly sweet after a spicy fish taco.

Cliff and I have learned small bits of the town's history, mostly from the ancient miners who took us on a tour down into the long-closed mine. We sit with our coffee, dazzled by the still-falling sun, the incredible light, the sense of history and deterioration alongside resurrection. We have been in town just four hours.

Up to the east are a couple of ancient worn hills, crowded with houses of many colors, precariously perched on earthen ledges. Some are shacks that were built during the days the mine was still open. There are still longtime residents who report the underground criminals and ghosts who are believed to be regular inhabitants. It's a wild stew of spirit and unreliable memory.

"Whcrc did you ever find this place?" I ask Cliff.

"Some useless travel guide, that finally had me with the line 'like Arizona one hundred years ago.' Turns out that's not quite it, but..." He looks around as if to explain everything that he can't describe. He takes my hand. "Before it gets totally dark, let's walk along Main Street to our place."

We stroll along the main street holding hands like two teenagers, stopping to be charmed by every darkened window display. Far from home, I imagine this is how

Vincent has felt, ordered to disappear, to accomplish some unknown plan, to be a stranger in foreign territory. I want to feel what he feels.

"Why did you bring me here?" I turn to Cliff. In a way, I'm calming myself with a question whose answer I don't need.

He stops to face me. "I wanted us to be in a place totally different from home, a place where anything can happen and whatever happens can be forgotten."

"Sounds like Las Vegas, but prettier and without the glitter."

"Las Vegas is a fraud, and this isn't." He lets go of my hand to approach the ancient door of our hotel.

We've checked in a couple of hours ago but only to drop off our bags. Our "place" is above one of the many galleries that are by now closed for the day. The building must be at least a hundred years old. The stairs are frighteningly steep but well lit. There are wide-plank floors and twelve-foot-high rooms. In our rustic bedroom, the windows are floor to ceiling, with lace panels providing privacy from Main Street. We climb the stairs in peaceful silence.

In our room, we collapse on th duvet that stretches across the king size bed. It has been a long travel day from New York to Tucson, and then a two-hour trip in the rented car to get here. "I wanted us to see this little town," Cliff says. "Don't know how long it will last, and I have no intention of coming this way again."

He moves closer and puts his arms around me. "Tomorrow at noon, my real job kicks in. So we have just a night here." He looks around the clean but rustic quarters. "At any rate, the hotel in Tucson will be a whole lot more elegant."

He is of course on bank business, some conference regarding changes in credit card usages and percentages. His call a week ago caught me off balance. His timing was perfect, school having closed for the summer only a couple of days before. I was still in organizing mode, but hoping to put together a plan for the luxury of a short vacation.

To be truthful, Erin's insistence that I "get out of town" had been a repeated tune running through my head for days. Cliff's invitation was the perfect response. His words were gentle and without pressure. "Kit, you know you need a break. You know you feel frightened and insecure in your apartment. I have a conference to attend in Tucson in a couple of days, and if you come along, I'll be able to enjoy it. We can make it a mini-vacation."

The silence from my end was no barrier, and he continued. "Kit, I'm not asking for anything you don't want to give. Share the few days with me, we'll catch up on old stories and old times. I expect nothing from you but your company. It's a change of wallpaper that both of us can use."

I roll over on the duvet, looking up at the wallpaper behind the bed. It's a roughly designed pattern, a darkened horizon with low shrubbery in the foreground sheltering a young antelope. It stands shaky on skinny legs, struggling to stay upright. Just at the edge of the greenery, quite close to her baby, is the mother, watching with a certain pride and looking as if she's about to encourage the fawn's efforts. She knows that in an hour her newborn will be steady on his feet, but she is obviously protective. In the distant shadows, only half visible, is some kind of large cat, too small to be a panther, too big to be a housecat. The entire picture is a bit ominous, makes me worry for the young one.

I murmur my ridiculous concern. Cliff answers with a gentle laugh. "It's a picture." He rolls a bit closer to my side of the bed and strokes my arm. "Whatever is going to happen isn't going to happen in the picture. Time is frozen as she protects her young. No harm can come to it as long as she is present." He runs his hand further up my arm and kisses my shoulder. "Make you feel better?"

"I feel fine," I say. "The picture just unsettled me for a minute."

He nuzzles my shoulder and then my neck. "See, the thing about this picture is that I see you and me."

"I don't quite follow. Are you about to tell me one of your famous fables?" This is so like him. I think of some of the tales he invented in college. He was famous for pointing out parallels and similarities between classmates and professors, and the characters we often read about. I find myself sliding into that distant past when he seemed as close to me as a second heart. I await his story.

"Okay, get this. You're the fawn and I'm the mama antelope. Her watch is intentional and a guarantee of safety. Antelopes are fast, and she can have that baby into the briars to where the cat can't reach them, in seconds." He leans back for a moment. "That cat has no idea about the trouble he'll have if he plunges into the thorns. He'll be a sorry feline, and they'll be home free."

He continues to kiss my throat and lick my lips. I squirm slightly, aware of the heat he's arousing; he stops to look at me. "Get it? You're the fawn, and I'm the antelope mom." I nod, of course I get it.

"You're insecure and need protection. Joseph lurks in the background, stalking and letting himself be seen. But you and I are going to save ourselves, because sooner or later, he'll find himself in a deadly situation that'll destroy him."

I'm speechless. Is he reading my mind? Does he know I dream of Joseph's death? The fable he has created comes before me as magic, not the silliness I first imagined. He knows me too well.

We are quiet for some time. Finally, he moves to a comfortable position lower on the bed. I remain still, trying to think of the protection he offers me. He continues his kissing, stroking, gentle nibbling until I think I'll lose my mind. When he finally clasps my hips to slide me under him, I slip my panties down below my knees. I'm lost by the time he asks if I have protection, and I nod, opening my legs in desperate longing for him.

"I won't do anything you don't want me to do," he whispers, and I tell him I want him to do anything he wants to do.

28

The morning light is slow coming up over the mountain, and we awaken later than we expect. I stretch luxuriously and turn toward Cliff, but he's already in the bathroom, as the sound of a spraying shower makes clear. He emerges, a towel wrapped around his lower torso. "Good morning, Kit." He leans to kiss me. I rise to greet him and get another, longer kiss.

He gestures to his half empty suitcase. "We should get back to Tucson. How about a quick breakfast at the coffee shop, and a once-in-a-lifetime visit to Tombstone, home of the OK Corral. It's on our way and shouldn't be missed." His sarcastic tone suggests this is not an incredible place to visit, but forever memorable just the same.

In the car, I ask him to refresh my distant memory about the OK Corral. I know it's about a gunfight between the law and the unlawful, but don't recall much else.

"Wait till we get there," he suggests, and starts laughing as he admits he can't remember either. We drive about forty minutes and run into a town that's unmistakably western. A rustic sign tells us in rustic letters that we're in Tombstone. Bar girls in ruffled dresses, drunks leaning against buildings, all constitute the atmosphere. I realize after a minute or two that they're actors.

At the OK Corral, we decide to watch the famous shootout, which will be showing in ten minutes. We wander along the wooden sidewalks, bumped into by children in costumes, native Americans in full regalia, and truly drunken old timers staggering out of bars. I'm entertained and curious at the same time.

Sitting on the bench in the Corral, I jump as the first shot explodes into the crowd. A cowboy sneaks out from behind a building. Then another, and another. Suddenly the enemies are facing one another and guns are blasting. Bodies go down as little kids cry or applaud, depending on their ages.

I am suddenly conscious of the guns before me. Of course these are replicas of antiques but I stare at them, wondering how a person would best operate one, wondering how the modern version would function. I know that what I've practiced with Ginger at the range looks nothing like these long-barreled six shooters. Cliff keeps turning to look at me, puzzled perhaps but not judgmental.

Finally, he asks outright, with a smile. "What's got your attention? You're making trigger motions every time a cowboy goes down. Practicing?" He endures my silence for a minute and stares at me. "You *are* practicing, aren't you?"

I sit on my hands and watch the show to the noisy end. Before the applause ends, Cliff ushers me out of the arena and into one of the quieter streets. "Okay, what am I missing? Are you mad at me again? Planning to shoot me?"

It's nothing," I say. But I'm suddenly trembling. Does part of me really want to kill Joseph? And is my obsession visible?

He asks again. "Are you upset with me? About last night?" He looks straight into my eyes. "Tell me, please."

"Of course not. It's not about you." I kiss him gently. "It was wonderful to be in your arms. I've been a bit edgy lately, feeling invaded and stalked. Sometimes I feel as if I'm walking on razors."

We walk back to the car. Cliff starts the engine with more noise and speed than usual and we head for Tucson, another hour or more ahead of us. He is very quiet. He taps his fingers on the steering wheel, either impatient or annoyed; I can't determine. We drive until the GPS says we have just a few miles to go.

"I didn't book two rooms for us. Is that okay?"

I look at him, incredulous. "We didn't have two rooms last night."

"Well, that was before you got all secret with me. I'm off balance, Kit. I know something's wrong but I can't untie the knot."

"Give me some time. Please. There are such crazy notions in my mind. Like buzzing bees, because they keep coming back and repeating the same things."

In the middle of Tucson's downtown, we thank the GPS and roll into the driveway of a mission-style hotel, all adobe walls and cactus. It's nine o'clock, too early to check in, but Cliff has a meeting in half an hour at one of the larger banks down the busy street.

We leave our bags in the lobby of the hotel and seek out the little coffee shop the woman at the reception desk has recommended. *The Beanery* is just a short walk away, in an elegant strip mall next to the hotel. It seems the other shops are still closed, but the window arrangements show a waterfall of riches that are out of my tax bracket.

"I'll take you on a shopping spree later," Cliff says. "Let's get the caffeine before I develop that snoring-while-walking syndrome."

The interior of the place is slick and appealing. The décor is a backdrop for the sale of silk scarves, Panama hats and gallery paintings. We admire the old Indian jewelry that borders the menu hanging just out of reach above us on the wall.

Seated with our coffees and a couple of corn muffins, we chat easily about where we've been and what we've seen. We agree Arizona has its own personality, maybe bi-polar but fascinating. I stare at a six shooter that hangs next to the jewelry. It's polished to a shine, as if it's never been used. I'm mesmerized by the gleam of the barrel and trigger, the balanced look of the gun, wondering how heavy it might be or how difficult to aim.

Cliff gently taps his teaspoon on the table. "Auditioning for 'Annie Get Your Gun'? You're showing signs of someone who needs a background check."

He's caught me off guard. I almost drop my coffee cup and catch it at the last minute, although it spatters a few drops on the table. I immediately try to remember who I am. "So sorry, I was just – uh – looking at the gun. It's an antique, I guess."

"This gun obsession is disturbing. Don't think I haven't noticed. I'm not kidding, Kit. What's up with that?" He sees my withdrawal and softens his voice. "I don't think you're planning to kill me. Or anyone else." He looks at me so carefully I feel that he's taking an X-ray. "Am I correct?"

"Oh, completely. I am definitely not planning to shoot you." I try to laugh but it's not working as well as I would like.

Cliff looks at his watch. "Got to go. Why don't you go back to the hotel, take a rest, then do some shopping? We can do further interrogation later." He takes a credit card out of his wallet, and hands it over to me as he smiles, kisses my lips and gathers the papers he has brought with him. "Card's limit is twenty-five thousand. See you in a couple of hours. Leave your phone on." I watch his easy walk as he heads toward a most impressive building down the street, smoothing his collar and tie.

29

Cliff comes back to the hotel with a small bouquet of white lilies; they're luscious and fragrant, if somewhat morbid. He fills one of the hotel coffee mugs with water, adds the flowers, and makes room for them on the night table. He hangs his suit jacket and tie on a convenient hook and removes his trousers so they can join the jacket on the hook. He catches me up in a sweeping hug, and lowers me gently to the bed. I roll closer to the edge so he can sit beside me. I don't need to, since he comes as close as possible to my side, making it our side.

We kiss. He begins to caress my face and throat, but retreats slightly. "You're looking at those lilies with a certain restraint," he says. "Don't you like them?"

"They're beautiful, Cliff. It's just that I associate lilies with death. All my life, I saw and smelled them at family services. Whether the deceased was old or young, lilies covered every surface in the funeral parlor."

"You've seen a lot of death, haven't you?"

"Probably not more than most. Close families celebrate events of every kind. I saw lots of weddings, too."

"Don't sidetrack me. I'm thinking of your parents, and of the horror stories you told me about your uncle's connections when we were still at Loreto. Remember how close we were?" He slips his fingers into my hair and pulls me closer.

"Of course. You were my counselor, my savior, in so many ways..." My words drift off as he quiets me with a deep, loving kiss.

"I can't wait to have you again," he whispers. "I'm going to undress you. We can talk about lilies later, if you want conversation."

"I don't want conversation. I just *want.*" I start to unbutton my blouse but he holds my wrist and uses his other hand to finish stripping me, of blouse, pants, a lacey wisp of underpants.

"Still no bra, huh? This is making my life way too easy." He runs his hand across my thighs and moves it into the space between my legs. I stay perfectly still, moaning slightly as he relentlessly strokes me until I come. "My turn," he whispers, and enters me so slowly that I think I might come again.

The flight home is easy. By this time, I have lost my inhibition about loving an old friend. We agree we will begin to spend time together that we should have started years ago.

I have an occasional twinge of guilt as Vincent works his sweet way into my mind, and I try to ease it by recalling our somewhat innocent love play. I'm reliving one of those tantalizing moments when Cliff breaks through the wall of my memory.

"What's on your schedule when you get home?"

I think for a full minute, not sure how much I want to reveal.

"It's a secret?"

"No secret. I have an appointment at High Noon Rod & Gun tomorrow afternoon."

He is nonplussed. He looks out the window, searching for a way to face this. "Geez, Kit. You're a different woman every time you speak. You make me wonder who you are. But tell me more."

I give him a brief outline of how I came to use the range, with a passing mention of Vincent's attempts to teach me how to protect myself. Cliff takes a sip of the water the attendant has provided. "Okay, now I get the gun mania. Tell you what. I'll meet you tomorrow at the range. Five o'clock. If this is your thing, I can make it mine."

I'm taken aback. "Oh no, we can't do that. I need to practice alone." I fumble for a lie that will discourage him. "I'm not permitted to bring a friend, it's too distracting."

"Fine. Those places have reputations that scare me, and should scare you. I won't enter, just wait for you outside. I'm not letting you go home alone."

The sudden sense of being protected burns. "Cliff, don't you remember the hour-long talks back at school, when I felt like my uncle's prisoner, when I had to fight for some form of independence and never really succeeded in escaping his power over me?"

He understands immediately. There's a long quiet moment before he finally speaks. "Kit, it's not power, it's love. I know I haven't used that word before, but I'm using it now. You're the most important person in my life. You were already that when we were at Loreto. When I lost you, I lost all feeling, all joy, all emotion. I let the work be my shell and I stayed inside it. These days we have just spent together –" He stops. "Look. I will never put you in a cage, or on a pedestal. You're your own person, and will always be. Okay?"

I put my arms around him as he whispers in my ear. "But I will be waiting for you tomorrow outside High Noon Rod & Gun."

The plane is landing. I adjust my seatbelt and shove my tote under the seat in front. There's no argument left in me. I take his hand and hold it tight as the pilot brings the plane home on a somewhat bumpy runway.

135

30

Dino is looking at me as if I'm out of my mind. "Not sure what you're asking me. You need a hit man? Stop playing with me and go do your practice. Jimmy's inside." He points toward the door to the range.

He's always good natured with me, sometimes in a crabby way. His attitude toward women hails from another generation, or maybe another century. Sure, they can practice shooting, he knows about the pioneer wives who protected their children, but everybody knows they were protected by big strong men. They aren't serious gun carriers. And they don't hire hit men.

What I have just said to him is innocent. It's a test. "Know somebody who needs a few bucks?"

He looks interested. "Sure, I know plenty of guys who could use a boost. What about it?"

I pretend to be kidding. "I want to get rid of somebody." This is the point at which he sends me through the door to the range.

He still hasn't let it go when I come back out an hour later. "Miss Gabrielli, I been thinking about what you said. Now, I know your Uncle Frank a long time. I respect him, we went through some hard times together years ago. Did he send you here to ask me that question?"

"About the 'few bucks'?"

"No, about getting rid of somebody."

"I didn't ask a question. I just said what I was looking for."

"So it's not from Frank?"

I lean closer over the counter to whisper to Dino. "It's probably the last thing my uncle would send me to ask. You were right, I was just kind of playing with you, you know?"

I can tell he doesn't want to let this go. I don't know if it's curiosity or the willingness to hook me up with somebody who needs the money.

"Ya know," he says, "I don't know if you're kidding, and I can't help you, but I can tell you one thing. A true thing. Really." He watches the expression on my face and repeats. "I mean it."

"So tell me."

"The person you could rely on, a guy who's been in the business a long time, who's true as gold, always delivers —" He reaches to tap my hand, to reassure me of the truth he's speaking. "Uh, you sure you want me to tell you?"

I look at a non-existent watch. "Dino, we've gotten this far. Spill it before I miss my train."

"Okay, but you won't tell nobody, right? Like I said, your uncle and me, we've been friends a long time, I don't want to cause him trouble, you know?"

"Dino, my next move is to the door," I turn slightly away from him, despite the fact that I'm as curious as a cat who hasn't heard about what curiosity does.

"Okay, okay." We lean toward one another like two love birds on a branch. By now, I'm holding my breath.

"It's Vincent," he whispers.

I wish I could ask him to repeat himself. I'm not sure I've heard clearly. Or maybe I'm sure but don't want to accept it.

"No," I say. "You've got the wrong person. Vincent's a locksmith, he works for my uncle. Can't be the same guy."

"That's my point, Miss Gabrielli, he's the person I just described. He's an expert about almost anything. Over the years, I've seen or heard of him taking down a number of people, people who were causing trouble, who went in the wrong direction, you know? Don't believe me, ask your uncle."

"No, it's fine. I understand. Thanks. See you, Dino, got to make my train. Catch you the next time. And thanks for the info."

I'm out of there and talking to myself, walking at a good clip toward the station. "My Vincent? Impossible. Not my Vincent." I'm thinking of his helpfulness, his tenderness, the tentative love-making that never happened. His green eyes.

What the hell is wrong with me, and why am I protecting him? Maybe he *is* a hit man, maybe he *has* taken down a herd of trouble makers. Why would that stop him from teasing me, trying to avoid anything serious between us?

I get it. He doesn't want to enrage my uncle by getting close to me, and is so disciplined he can manage his self control. On the R train, I shed a tear or two. I feel used and betrayed that he fears my uncle more than he wants me.

I stop short to remind myself I am in love with Cliff. What the hell is wrong with me, I ask myself again. I have no answer to the question. Cliff catches up with me, and together we head for the subway station, in a silence that suits both of us perfectly.

31

The letter comes in the regular mail. No handwritten note stuffed in the mail slot, simply a stamped envelope that looks as if it could be a notice, or a bill, or an invitation to something important. But still, it looks peculiarly personal. I stumble upstairs in the growing darkness, place my school work on the table, and settle on the couch with my handful of mail.

I sort through the usual pleas for money, the reminders of bargains not to be missed, the political surveys. I toss them on the cushion beside me. I take the last envelope in hand and slip the letter opener under the seal. I remove a lengthy, carefully printed letter with some glued ads attached as part of an included message. A few sentences along, I drop the sheet of paper and sit down, my gut in my throat as I try to decide what to do with it.

The letter is both strange and threatening, laughable and frightening. Joseph has used familiar expressions stolen from ads, and has used them to get his point across. Each of them is a quotation cut from a catalog or newspaper. But next to each quotation appears his hand written message.

'Explore the world' becomes "I'll explore your heart."

'Instant rewards' expresses his opinion of how I will feel when he can enjoy my body again.

'Discover more' claims "I want to discover your pussy again."

'Thirst quenching' describes how satisfying it will be for him to drink the wetness of my aroused affection.

141

'*Most spectacular*' assures me "You have the most spectacular body."

'*A must*' indicates his need, his agony, to see me soon.

He uses '*Rugged and ready*' to describe in detail his eagerly awaiting penis, which the next insert describes as '*Better than ever.*'

I am repulsed and terrified. He is crazier than I can ever recall or imagine. The letter ends with his longing to be with me again, with his conviction that all we have to do to create the perfect life together is to enjoy an unforgettable reunion. For this he includes a future date and the assurance that he will appear on the listed day, several weeks ahead. My throat closes with anxiety and the recognition that I can't live a normal life as long as I wait for him to make good his promise.

The questions fly. Will I have to contact my uncle, should I report this horror to Cliff, can I handle it myself? I check every lock and window sash. I go to bed, trembling, with my pink Ruger under my pillow. Loaded, just as Vincent left it.

During the night, I dream of an angel disguised as a thief. The angel is in my bedroom, examining my possessions and putting desired objects under her wings. She opens a map and points me to a street I've never seen before. "You must listen," she insists. "It will call you." I feel more secure when I awaken, but still under a dangerous cloud.

32

At first I don't recognize the chimes that awaken me. I roll over, alone and confused, when suddenly I see the church steeple outside my back window and hear the bells again. Of course. Church bells! The angel! I produce a fuzzy smile in a moment of disorientation that turns into a feeling of safety.

I've awakened in my new apartment in Brooklyn Heights, a few short blocks from the promenade. Cliff has donned his savior cape, the role he has performed often in the past. He has taken it on himself to cut his regular hours at work to help me find an affordable place to live before the insane deadline threatened by Joseph.

The day I showed Cliff the letter was the day we began our search with every broker he knew. At first, I was overwhelmed by his kindness. My repeated gratitude annoyed him. With gentle modesty, he shut me up. "I can take a half day off. I'm the boss's son."

It's striking how quickly we fall back into the kind of relationship we had at Loreto. We take long walks, appraising different streets, admiring stunning historic houses, checking the distance to transportation options. We sit for hours on the promenade, watching Lady Liberty, wondering if she's watching us. In this late summer weather, we stop for iced coffee and bring it back to the Henry Street apartment we have agreed is a good rental choice.

It's a second floor studio, the back half of a renovated brownstone. The single room is large, with two oversized windows overlooking the back yard and garden of the church behind my building. There's a kitchen the size of an old-time phone booth. The two-burner hot plate and half refrigerator are literally tucked inside a closet, along with a mini-triangle of a sink. The single cabinet is so high up in the closet I can't reach it. The first day, Cliff and I discover stirrups along the door frame, which can be folded down to allow me access to the cabinet. I feel as if I'm in the circus, balancing on a piece of braced metal and backing down from it, carrying a dish or a glass with a certain precarious grace.

It's smaller and more expensive than my old apartment, but the thrill of all this is the sense of safety I live with. I have forwarded the mail, changed my phone number, stocked the new apartment's tiny pantry. I have as yet told no one where my new digs are. Cliff and I have moved the few pieces of furniture I treasure with the help of his dad's pickup truck, driven all the way from Saratoga.

I feel content. Cliff and I spend seductively luscious evenings together. Sometimes he stays late into the night, making love to me until we are both exhausted. I am, however, accustomed to being alone, and I do not encourage him to stay overnight.

33

My next step is to inform Uncle Frank. Cliff and I practice my script in a way that will not anger my uncle. I know he will be offended that I have made this move without his knowledge. As the patriarch of the family, he is supposed to make these decisions, direct the process, give his seal of approval. I decide to make an appointment with him at Café Blue and invite him to Henry Street if he seems willing. My aim is not to exclude him; I do want him to know where I am living. But I don't want him to think he can run my life.

When I call my uncle, I get a confusing voice mail. Something about leaving one's number, but with an additional message that mentions his absence from the country at this time, and an inability to return calls. I'm in no hurry to meet him, but just the same, I call Aunt Mary to get the real deal.

She insists I come to her Bay Ridge home for a visit, unwilling to discuss this on the phone. "You know how it is with the family," she says. "There's really nothing I can tell you. Especially since I don't know anything. See you tomorrow afternoon. About three thirty is best." She disconnects the call, assuming I will be available when it's convenient for her. And of course, I will be.

She's waiting for me on the front porch, busily knitting one of her many scarves. It's a beautiful day, cool and dry, suggesting that summer's humidity is coming to an end. She sees me coming down the street, and puts away her handwork.

"Sit here," she says, "next to me." She pats the cushion on the chair to her left. "So you tried to reach your uncle?"

"Couldn't actually make contact. He seems not to be available right now, if I understood the message."

"Well, that message isn't particularly clear," she acknowledges. "Tell you the truth, it's not supposed to be useful." She looks clear into my eyes. "You understand?"

"So it's the usual family rule, double talk?"

"We don't really call it that. It's a way to keep strangers at a distance. And a way to protect the family."

"Okay. I get that. But what exactly are you protecting? Is there a problem? Are we in trouble?"

When she doesn't answer, I offer more options. "Is the IRS on our trail? Did one of the casinos collapse?"

"Kitty, you're taking this much too lightly. Your uncle is in a tight spot at the moment. He will eventually work his way out of it, as he has done in the past. It's not something to laugh about, but neither is it something to ignore. Capisce?"

I shift in my chair, and look out into the street. Quiet gardens, clean driveways, meticulously mowed lawns. Everything seems so harmless. But I know better. Nothing about my uncle is harmless.

"So what do I do now? I want to let him know I've moved. I no longer felt safe in the apartment after so many scares, so Cliff and I found another place."

"What do you mean by 'scares'?" She seems genuinely clueless, and I feel obliged to explain.

"The apartment was invaded, Joseph held me prisoner, more than once..."

She stares at me, picks up her knitting for comfort. "Why didn't I know this? When did it happen?"

"I didn't discuss this with you. What was the point? Uncle Frank didn't even believe me, totally denied the possibility that Joseph could do anything without his

146

knowledge. Remember the conversation we had, during which he assured you I was being childish and delusional?"

She nods. "I had stored that away. It seemed so without reason, and all I wanted to do was spare Frank any worry."

"Okay, so how do I let him know I've moved?" Sarcasm edges its way in. "Without worrying him, of course."

I can see she's distraught. She resumes massaging her fabric, twisting the fragile material between her fingers, trying to straighten out the issue we've turned into a knot.

"So is he in danger?"

"We don't know exactly. He's far enough away from home to be well hidden, and I pray every day that he's safe."

"When do you expect to make contact again?"

She changes the subject as secretly and tactfully as she has learned to be over the years. "When I do, I'll explain your move to him. I'm sure he'll be understanding. You moved because you wanted something more convenient, right?"

"Yeah, you could say that." I pulled my little black book out of my purse and scribbled my new address. "Here's the info. Thanks, Aunt Mary."

She gets up from her chair. "Thanks for the visit," she smiles. "It means so much to me to see you. Now that you're grown, we hardly see one another."

Great routine, I think to myself. She hasn't told me a damn thing, but she's getting me off Frank's back. Ah, family.

"Take care, Aunt Mary. See you soon." I bend over to get kissed on both cheeks, and wave when I reach the sidewalk. I wave until I can't see her clearly anymore. I know she's still on the porch, probably praying over her knitting.

34

It's four days before school will actually start, but some of the more ambitious or curious students stop by to determine who their teacher will be, or what their schedules will be. I've picked up mail addressed to Georgia Trent, which I'll deliver to her today. She's just back from a trip to visit her mother in Trinidad. In our phone call this morning, she asked me to pick up her school mail and bring it to her at her apartment, just a few blocks away. I'm still shuffling the mail when I catch Becca's voice at the door.

"Miss G, I saw your boyfriend again today! He was just outside!" Becca comes shooting into the empty room, excited beyond breathing. "He was right there. He waved at me!"

"Who waved at you?" I am having trouble absorbing her report.

"You know, that boyfriend who was 'last one in' that time, and then he kissed you, I remember."

"Oh, Becca, he's not my boyfriend, and he should not be near our school. Remember, we threatened to call the police because he was trespassing."

"Oh," she says, her bubble slightly punctured. "Well, he was outside, and he waved."

"It's okay, Becca. Thank you for letting me know. I'll be sure he's gone before any of you are ready to leave."

"Okay, Miss G. I'm going straight home now. And I won't wave if I see him."

I wait until I'm sure the few girls who were in the

building are gone. I stalk out of the building in a rage. I'm muttering to myself, planning my moves if I happen to see him. I'll call the police and mention my Order of Protection. They probably can't do more than check with Family Court to prove my assertion, but it will humiliate him and piss him off. I'm so angry my hands tremble, but I don't see a sign of him.

I realize suddenly that I've left Georgia Trent's mail back in my classroom. I nearly trip in my hurry to get back before the janitor locks up. I have my own keys, but it's a hassle to open the main door. I breathe easier when I see the side door still ajar, and head for my room in a hurry.

I snatch the mail from my desk, and examine a red envelope I don't recall seeing earlier. It's sealed, but has no address. I lift it as if it were a dead mouse. I look for a place to destroy it, but my curiosity wins. I separate the envelope from its contents.

There is a red heart made of velvet, with "forever" written on it. A plastic snack bag has something in it I can't identify, until I look closer. It's a white powder, probably talcum, but it looks frighteningly like – please, no – anthrax. I don't open it, but I take it with me to the nearest precinct and hand it to the woman at the desk.

"Former boyfriend left me a message," I say. "Still screwing up my life."

I tell her Joseph's name. I can't provide an address. She takes my vital statistics, my ID, the names of two references and asks for my driver's license, an item I haven't got. "You'll have to provide finger prints," she says calmly, and sends me to the appropriate corner of the room. She wraps the envelope in some aluminum bag that could probably hold the Constitution, and sends it down a chute, where I'm sure it will be subject to chemical examination.

Back at the desk, my fingerprints on record forever, I return to the front desk. "Can I go?"

"Yeah, checked with one of your references about your ID. Don't leave town. We'll contact you about the powder. Or stop by in a day or two. You'll be under surveillance from here on in."

This sounds way too much like a cheap movie. I make my way out to the street, on my way to Georgia's apartment. I look around, wondering if I'm already under surveillance. Does it mean I'm being watched, or protected? One sounds better than the other, I think, just as I catch a glimpse of a nicely dressed handsome man turning a corner some yards ahead of me. His gait is uncomfortably familiar, and I increase my speed to sneak a look around the corner. There's no one to be seen.

Picking up my speed to the next street, I recognize the building Georgia described to me over the phone. It's an apartment cooperative, having had a makeover a couple of years ago. The facade is polished stone and rather chic. The doorman lends a touch of elegance, looking sharp in his dark suit and holding his position outside the two marble steps to the entrance. He delivers a broad smile when I approach him. I tell him my name and he nods knowingly. "I'm Bryon, Miss, and yes, ma'am, I've been waiting for you. I'll call up to Miss Georgia." His phone already at his ear, he touches my elbow and guides me into the lobby. "Elevator's right here," he gestures. "Fourth floor."

By the time the elevator door slides open, Georgia is waiting for me in front of an open door down the hall. She looks travel worn but presents her usual smile. "Come on in, have a cup of tea. I'm ready to collapse and I need sane company. Love my mom, but spending a week with that crew... Well, come on in."

The kitchen is fresh and simple, the walls painted a pale lemon, the sheer white curtains admitting plenty of light. She motions me to sit at a small round oak table that's polished to a glow. Two tea cups have crisp white napkins beside them, and an etched glass jar hosts a handful of silver spoons. There's a kettle starting to whistle on the stove.

Georgia reaches into the compulsively neat pantry, and comes out with a box of shortbread cookies. The wrapping reveals a picture of a fat little dog. I recognize the brand, and I think of my uncle beheading the shortbread Scotty dog in my living room. Why does he come so easily to mind?

Georgia gives me a handful of tea bags and asks me to choose one. I pick up one that says 'Calm and Peaceful,' and lower it into my cup. She laughs. "You, too? When I got in, I grabbed one that says 'For Therapy.' The titles don't really matter, they're all good, herbal, organic. Whatever that means." She shrugs. "Guess I read too many labels."

She settles next to me at the table and shakes her head. "Travel wrecks me. At least the trip down there does, you know what I mean? My mom cries the minute she sees me. She makes phone calls. There arrive too many weeping cousins and babies, aunts and their crawling toddlers. Even grandma cries like a baby. Everybody wants something from me. 'What did you bring me?' Don't get me wrong, I love children. But I deal with them all year at work, all sizes, some sensitive, some just the most lovable children I ever will see." She stops for a breath. "But I have enough of them that I don't need more when I visit my mom."

"I think I understand," I say. "I have only a bunch of old aunts whose behavior isn't any different. Only difference, they don't crawl, they just whine. And then there's my uncle. Certainly not a whiner, but a boss. Runs my life like it's a race track."

Georgia raises her eyebrows. "Meaning too fast?"

"No, not exactly. He picks the runners and calls the winners. Know what I mean?"

"He have something to do with your ex, the guy who asked after you that day at school?"

"He has something to do with everyone, but yes, my ex

works for him. Or so I'm told."

She settles back in her chair. "None of my business, none of it. But let's hear the story. You've been carrying a heavy burden for a while, that's obvious. Want to tell me about it?"

I think to myself, where do I start?

"Start at the beginning," she reads my mind. "I'll just listen."

So I do, and she does.

By the time Georgia knows my story, it is getting dark. The afternoon has disappeared into dusk and shadows. She has assured me that school will be safe, that she'll arrange a more frequent security schedule, and the guards will be notified regarding the order of protection.

Another feeling of safety comes in a quick call from the precinct. The woman who calls speaks gently but to the point. She asks first for ID information I gave to her earlier. Then, "The material you submitted turned out to be corn starch," she says. "Do you want it returned?"

"Mmm, let me think it over. I don't think so," I reply. We both laugh aloud, which requires Georgia to beg the question. She is still shaking her head when my tale is done.

I gather my few belongings and, after a grateful hug, head for the door. "It's past eight. The time flew. Can't thank you enough, Georgia, for listening, and for supporting me."

"You're thinking of leaving in the dark? It's safe enough these days, but you don't know where he is and whether he's waiting for you."

I admit her words frighten me, but I can't be afraid forever. "No worries, Georgia. The A train goes directly where I have to go, with just one change. If something alarms me, I can always take a cab."

"I know you're a big girl. But you trust too much. So be careful, know what's around you, and don't relax your observation skills, okay?"

The doorman is as charming as he was earlier. "Good evening, Miss. I hope you had a pleasant time with Ms. Trent. You know, she chatted with me earlier today, and she was looking forward to your visit."

"Thank you, Bryon. We had a lovely time."

"There was a young man asking about you," he says. I freeze in place. "I didn't tell him not a thing," he reassures me. "He wanted to know what floor you were on, and I made it clear I'm not in a position to reveal such information."

"What did he want?"

"Never got that far, Miss. He finally strolled away. The only thing I heard, was him talking to himself that now he knows where you live. Believe me, I didn't bother to correct him." He looks at me for approval.

"Bryon, you did the right thing." I glance up and down the street. "Would you call me a cab, please?"

"Certainly, Miss. You can wait inside. I'll call you when the taxi's here."

~ ~~

The cab driver plays quiet music, there's little traffic, and I'm foolishly elated. So Joseph thinks he knows where I live. He has somehow followed me all the way to Georgia's and believes he knows something that isn't true. It gives me hope that I can keep him out of my life for a while, until the next time.

I can hardly wait to get back to my one-room apartment in the Heights. I look forward to it as if it were a castle, where I am the Queen. I pray the King will be there as well. I'm already smiling when the cab pulls up to my address, thinking of the welcome Cliff will have ready for me. I tip the cabbie a ridiculous amount and he waits till I'm safely inside the building.

The apartment is pitch black. Even the night light isn't on. When I flip the switch, it's clear that there's no one at home but me. At first I'm surprised. Then I'm worried. Cliff is always here before dark, and it's already after nine. He stays late, but respects my need to be alone, waiting sometimes until eleven or midnight before he leaves.

He usually has some wonderful game to play with me. He pretends to be an investigator, sent by the police to respond to a neighbor's complaint. He undresses me slowly, looking for contraband, stolen money or drugs. Or he hands me what looks like a wad of money, calls me a whore, and takes me, claiming what he has paid for. We laugh a great deal, mostly after we've made other noises that are equally lovely and satisfying.

But now there's no sign of him. He has the key and sometimes I find a note, if not a phone message. I find neither. Perhaps there's been a late night meeting at the bank, or at some restaurant that serves late into the night. I hope he hasn't had too much to drink. I try to sleep and decide to contact him in the morning.

It's a long and restless night. By the time the day has shed early light through the tall rear windows, I decide to meet him outside the bank that afternoon when he leaves work. I get through my day expecting a call that never comes, but I'm prepared to embrace him later, sure that some unexpected event has interfered with our reunion.

35

I'm sitting on an iron bench down the street from the bank entrance, alert to every man who might be the one I'm waiting for. At shortly after 5:00 p.m., a wave of men and women begins to spread out into the street, the various streams separating as they head for one subway station or another, or wait for the car that will meet them.

I rise from the bench, watching for Cliff. I see no one who resembles him. I must have missed him, or he hasn't yet left his post. What's next? I ease myself through the revolving door, to be stopped by a kind security guard.

"Sorry, Miss, the bank is closed to the public at the moment. If you can stop by tomorrow, it's open late, until 9:00, but today's the early closing."

"I'm looking for someone who works here. Can I speak to a receptionist who might be able to tell me if he's gone?"

"I'm sorry, Miss, the bank's officially closed. If there are some folks still inside, they can't deal with the public. It's a safety regulation, you understand." He politely maneuvers me to a position at which I can re-enter the revolving door, this time toward the sidewalk. "Have a nice evening, Miss." As I walk slowly away, I see him secure the door so it can no longer revolve.

Disturbed, worried, and unsure, I start walking to regain my equilibrium, but with no destination in mind. The streets are crowded, adults released from a day's work the way children escape at the end of school. People choose their own rhythms, some at a marching pace, some recovering some of the energy they've left behind at the job.

Everyone seems to have a goal. I am the only one without one.

I turn several corners at random and suddenly see a familiar landmark. On the next corner I see a sign I've seen before: *The Silent Bean.* A wave of relief flows over me, as I look forward to hiding out with a mocha in a quiet corner, perhaps asking Sabina if she's seen Cliff. I cling to that as the hope I've been living with.

I carry that hope even further. Perhaps, I fantasize, Cliff will be in the coffee shop, waiting for me. I am still on the sidewalk, a statue among moving crowds, when I see a couple leaving *The Silent Bean.* She is petite, blond and beautiful. She's wearing a dark blue dress, knee length with a slit to the thigh, and a V neckline that ends at the waist. It reveals just about everything a guy – or any passersby - would want to get a look at. He is wearing a three-piece suit and carrying a briefcase. They walk out into the masses, his arm around her waist, her head inclined onto his shoulder. I'm dumbfounded, but not confused. I would know Cliff anywhere.

The phone call comes early that evening. Cliff speaks lovingly, as if he were concerned. "Oh, I'm so glad you're back. I thought you were staying overnight with Mrs. Trent."

"No, I came home late last night, to find you were not here."

"Yeah, my loss. As I said, I somehow thought you wouldn't be back till late tonight. Got my calendar screwed up."

What he's saying makes no sense. If he thinks I'd be home tonight late, why is he calling now? "Well, I'm here now, and missing you," I say. "How soon can you come?"

"That's the bitch of it. I assumed you'd be home way late, so I planned a meet with several of the new interns. I actually worked already last night with a couple of them, and will see the newbies tonight. Show them the ropes, go through some of the routines, do a tour of the building, so they'll feel comfortable when their schedule starts."

"Yes, I'm sure they'll learn a great deal from you."

"Listen, I'll rush over tomorrow when I'm done for the day. Can't wait to see you. Can't wait to be with you."

"Can hardly wait," I say, and wonder if he can hear my smile. I'm not sure if I'm laughing at myself, or his lies. Neither one is terribly funny.

36

I set out midmorning to *The Silent Bean*, taking advantage of my free time, and avoiding the busy morning rush. I find one of the shop's quiet corners, order an Americano and a scone for breakfast. I grab one of the magazines on the counter, wanting to look preoccupied instead of crazy.

I review yesterday's experience, an ongoing nightmare and puzzle. Could I be off base, misinterpreting what I saw? She could be a new intern, or a new girlfriend. Or both. I recall his arm around her waist and her cuddling into his shoulder. She could be a dear cousin. I need to work this out. I want to discuss this with Cliff tonight, but I don't want to do it in hysterics or fury.

Sabina waves as she steps behind the bar, directing her assistant to go out the back door to the supply room. I wave back. When the young man returns with a giant package of what could be napkins, he begins to unwrap and arrange things on the service counter. I watch his meticulous rhythm, and admire his youthful good looks.

Sabina walks slowly over to me, and sits beside me. "How's it going? You look to be in deep thought."

"I guess you could say that."

"Enjoying your summer break?"

I decide not to fib. "It has its moments."

She shifts in her seat. "You look unsettled."

I don't reply, but she reads my face. "Is it him?"

I raise my eyes to hers. Do I dare ask about him? I hesitate, but I don't have to say a word, as she clears her throat and looks distractedly out the front window. She's going to tell me. "Excuse me if you think I'm gossiping. It's info I believe you deserve to know. May I continue?" I nod, choked by fear and anger.

"Well, the thing is this. I could say he's a nice enough young man, but his family is very influential; they carry a lot of weight. He wants to please them, especially his father. There's this colleague at the bank who has a daughter, this gorgeous blonde, and Cliff's father has pushed hard to bring them together." She stops to watch my reaction.

"Yes, I think I saw them together yesterday. But Cliff has been with me for some time, our relationship is exciting and loving. We've travelled together, we've spent nearly every night together..."

She broke into my story. "But he doesn't stay overnight, does he?"

I fumble for words. "No. I- I like my privacy, I need time to do my work, I- I tell him not to stay. It's been my idea, not his, that he leaves me."

"Apparently, the schedule plays right into his dilemma. His father invites the colleague almost every night for dinner, the daughter tags along, and they stay late enough for Cliff to get to know her. She's a beauty, she's a flirt, and her Dad's worth millions. Perfect recipe for the soup you're in right now."

"But he loves me." That's as far as I get in my reply.

"Sure, he does. But he doesn't know what love is. He was your friend for so long, he feels he knows you inside out. But there's still your friendship he can fall back on, without calling it love. She, on the other hand, is not his friend, she's his temptation. And that's much more exciting. And the fact that his father encourages the relationship makes it more difficult, and appealing. Cliff has sought his father's approval since he was in kindergarten. It's the way the family always functioned."

I reach for straws. "What about his mom? Has she got

anything to say?"

"Pft! She doesn't play any role but showing off her clothes."

"But his parents met me. They met me several times. It was when we were still in school, a few years ago, and they *liked* me. I know it."

"Honey, there's an approval issue at large here. They didn't know yet that you were, and still are, a mobster's niece."

I look around for negative evidence. I have neither excuse nor truth that could change their position.

"Sabina, how do I know this whole story's true?"

"Well, just wait to see how the show ends, and who's still in the cast."

We are both silent for a minute. "Sabina, what can I do?"

"Depends on how dignified you want to be. Throw a tantrum in front of his family, or in front of the girl, and you've proven your middleclass lack of savoir faire in your need to confront him." She shrugs. "Or, tell him you know of his betrayal, and give him an option to make a grownup choice."

"Makes me uncomfortable...I don't really know what he'd choose."

"That says a lot about the relationship, doesn't it?"

I bow my head. A few minutes later, I rise from my chair and enclose Sabina in a warm hug. "I'll be in touch. Thank you."

37

I wander the apartment in my pajamas, depressed, angry and irrational. I know Cliff well enough to believe he loves me. I think of every night we spent together, of his tenderness, his games, our travels together, his need for me, and his lovemaking that magnified my need for him. I cannot picture my life without our sexual pleasures. I felt they made me beautiful, to Cliff and to myself.

I thought we'd always be together. Facing the odds that are in front of me now is painful and unbelievable. No imagination can convince me I can win this war. The weapons are money, status and someone else's beauty. I laugh at myself when I think of my desire to have Joseph dead. I'd gladly switch the wish to this blonde who has attacked my world.

I search for more mature strategies.

At about five, I take a shower and dress myself. He will be here soon if he comes from work. I choose a silky dress, one that he admired some months ago. It clings to the body, revealing my slender curves and highlighting their accessibility. Will it awaken his memories of us together? Will it melt the distance between us?

But I remind myself he does not know anything about my insecurity, nor does he have an inclination that I have the information Sabina passed on to me. I have to play my role of eager lover, attentive friend, agreeable listener. I can pull it off, and I will.

He comes in the door, handsome in jeans and a sweat shirt, carrying a huge bundle of fresh flowers, roses mixed with lilies. "Picked them up on the way here. Tried to find some with all lilies, no luck." He smiles at his own sarcasm and gives me a quick kiss.

I am comforted that he recalls my discomfort with lilies. His concern, and his gift of flowers, are already soothing my fear. This is the man I know and love. He puts the flowers in the sink, runs cold water in the basin. He removes the lilies one by one, lays them aside and immerses the roses. The gesture is childishly appealing.

He moves to embraces me. The kiss is long and breathtaking. "I was so worried about you," I whisper into his shirt. "I couldn't find you, and when you did call, it was nearly two days since we'd seen one another."

"Yeah. I screwed that up. Guess I missed the mailman on that one."

"Where were you that first night? I got home about eight thirty and the apartment was dark." I clench my fists and await a reply.

His tone is abrupt. "I told you. The interns."

"Yes. But no note, no message, I was really worried."

"What are you, some kind of baby? So you spent a whole night by yourself. I've never known you to be afraid of the dark."

"Not when you're with me. Besides, I wasn't afraid, I was alone." I'm pushing my case, and he's getting impatient.

"Look, Kit. I had something else to do. I made a mistake, I didn't notify you. I thought you were spending the night with your Mrs. Trent."

"There was never a reason to think that. We never discussed it, and I certainly wasn't planning to stay out late the following night. What was on your calendar that second night?"

"Kit, you're getting out of line. I have a life outside of ours. It was business, I was working late."

"Is that why you called me that next night to say you thought *I'd* be late? Another ridiculous assumption. So you could have another free night?"

"Okay, look." He pulls me over to the couch and sits me down next to him, hard. "Obviously you're not going to accept any old story. I'm going to tell you something you can't discuss with anyone. Never. You understand?"

I'm starting to sweat. I nod.

He rises from the couch and paces a few steps, returns and sits next to me. "It's your uncle. I work for him once in a while."

"You what? My uncle? Doing what?" I can barely put words together. "You hardly know him." My world is spinning. I was expecting to hear about the blonde.

"Know him well enough. Got familiar after we left school. There was some investment class I addressed at the bank and he showed up with some guy. On the way out, he approached me. He remembered me with you, asked about my job, and that led to talking about my father, who brought me into the banking world."

"You didn't tell me..." I remind myself that my uncle has never told me of the connection, either.

"There wasn't much to tell, not at first. He liked to talk about banking and investing and every other thing that connected to money, and how to double it. He was a quick student."

"What did he want to learn? I thought he already knew every way to make or steal a fortune"

"C'mon, Kit. People like him are never done. Making more is what keeps them breathing."

"So you helped him."

Cliff gets up again to pace. He takes a few steps and comes back to stand in front of me. "It didn't cost me anything to be helpful."

"So you continued until it would cost *him* something."

He shrugs. "It's money, Kit. I'm a banker. I learn more about this business every ten minutes. And your uncle has taught me things I would never have been ready for."

"How do you mean?"

He hesitates. "You know we can't spread any of this, don't you?"

The phrase chills me. It reminds me of the drama in Boston, the request that asked me to keep another secret. I hear Seppi's voice, his remark that my uncle would want me to keep Seppi's business quiet, to bury it, as he put it.

"I understand. What am I being asked to keep to myself? All you've told me is my uncle started as your student and then became your teacher. What else came of this?"

Cliff clears his throat and reaches out to my hand. "The fact that you're his niece has played a role, as you can imagine. I love you and feel the need to tell you all this. Making you part of the secret will actually keep us together."

What he's saying sounds insane. Is he really saying I have earned his affection because I'm Frank's niece? Or is he saying I should keep silent because Frank is my uncle? Or am I protecting Cliff because of all I've heard just now, which isn't very much.

"What is 'all this' as you call it?"

"Does it disturb you?"

"Damn right. Suddenly, your relationship with my uncle is more important than ours."

Cliff is silent for a long time, until I finally get up and make a pot of coffee. I come back with my cup. I offer one, but he declines. "Can't swallow anything right now." He puts his head in his hands.

I wait till my cup is empty. I walk over to him and caress his face. He moves back a little, still apparently in his own world. Finally, he asks me to sit beside him again.

"The thing about secrets can solve this whole thing. All you need to know is I make a good living at the bank. But I make an enormous living outside of that."

I sit still, confused.

"If I continue to work with Frank, I will get richer. But I want to include you in the situation, because you're my safety net. He appreciates the situation because he values you. If you know what I'm talking about, you'll want to protect not just me, but your uncle, too. Because what happens to him will affect us always. Is that making any sense?"

It doesn't. I say, "I think so. Maybe."

He gets up. "Let's fuck and put this stuff on the shelf. We can talk more later. I want to have you. It's been too long." He starts to remove my shoes. I feel something besides desire, something more like unsteady reassurance. I pull my silky dress over my head.

38

It's eight o'clock, darkening night, when Cliff rolls out of the bed. He showers and dresses, pulling his jeans up as he exits the bathroom. "Got to go," he reaches for his shirt and looks at his watch. "Have several calls to make, business issues."

"You can call from here, can't you?" He's been here only a couple of hours, and I am reluctant to let him go.

"Kit, no. None of it will make sense to you, anyway."

"But I'd feel part of your life. I won't listen, I'll just take comfort in your trust. Please... You've told me a hardly believable tale about my uncle's role in your life, you made clear I'm a part of something I don't even understand. And now you say you can't even make a phone call I might overhear."

He breathes an exasperated sigh. "Okay, okay, I'll make a couple of calls if it makes you feel better. The rest I'll make on my way home. That good enough?"

I nod, ashamed of my childish insistence. He is already absorbed in the first call.

I retreat to the bathroom, and run the water. When I turn it off, I hear only a few words, and I understand the context of none of them. Words like *arrangement, connection, middle man,* and others make it boringly businesslike. I try not to put sentences together but I am a woman and can't help myself. This first call is brief, obviously to a colleague, the topic disposed of in a few seconds. I am still in the bathroom, but with the door ajar.

When the second call begins, Cliff's voice seems more

intense. It's unavoidable that I hear some of it. "Yes, I told them," he sounds annoyed. "Put it on the line and pay the guy. Cops take money for trivia, and that's what this is." There is a silence. Then, a few words more. "Look, Seppi's the go-to guy. He knows the rules, we don't have to know anything about it. Just provide the payout."

My mouth gets dry. I swallow what feels like sand. I stand before Cliff in my pajamas, speechless. I swallow again. "Who was that?"

"Just one of your uncle's connections. Nothing important, not to you, anyway. Same old stuff, about who does what, and when. Look, I have to get going, more calls to make, more deals to close." He bends to kiss me. "Think of your uncle's business, spilling profits in our laps. We're going to be rich." He laughs and heads for the door. I follow him like a three-year-old toddler. I accept his embrace, hug him in return. When the door closes, I slide to the floor. I doubt that I will sleep well this night.

By morning, I have completed the puzzle. Some pieces are missing, but the pattern is clear. My lover is investing in a project my uncle supports. I want to think Cliff does not know the nature of the project, but he certainly knows the illegal moves that keep it going: the pay offs, the bribes, the coverage that allows the event to take place. I wonder if he also knows about the introduction to sex for barely pubescent girls, who pay for this experience and spread its excitement among their envious friends.

I leave my bed to make a pot of coffee and cannot drink a drop. At least twice, I take a mouthful and spit it into the sink. How can I handle this? For one thing, it's information I'm not supposed to know. Even further, it's information I dare not even share. I recall Seppi telling me my uncle would want me to bury my knowledge of the scheme. As childhood friends, they have a bond. Such a bond means silence, secrecy about all things. There is no compromise, there is only revenge. And I am now part of the bond.

So is Cliff. This is the friend who saw truth as the answer to everything when we were college students. Even after graduation, Cliff believed his job to be upright and based on integrity, so he said. While we were still friends, I heard much from him about the meticulous way the system worked. It was soothing to know this. Then, as we became lovers, he continued to bring me into the culture of finance, explaining it could not be run without straightforward honesty.

I shudder now to think I believed it all. But I didn't know exactly when he and my uncle had signed their unholy contracts.

39

I need to be at school for only a few hours, preparing for the opening. By the time I get home, I have made a decision. I can't face Cliff right now. Does he know about these little girls, doped and raped and grateful for the experience, victims of Seppi's illegal, repulsive operation?

It becomes impossible for me to visualize sharing conversation, intimacy and sex with him. His interests have wrapped themselves around nothing but money, and he doesn't seem to care how it's packaged. He has spoken of huge cuts and profits from Frank's business, but I did not put the puzzle together soon enough to understand the source of such riches.

I pick up the phone and dial the number that will probably connect me with Cliff's voice mail. I'm cowardly, unwilling to struggle through a conversation. The call goes directly to voice mail, where I leave my message. I don't say I need a break, I lie instead. I tell him I am taking the girls on a field trip, a four-day exchange with another school. We will take the bus to Maine, and then spend our time exploring Eastport, the most easterly town in Maine. We will let him know when we return.

Although I have no intention of going anywhere but to school, it is a trip I have made with students once before. Should Cliff ask me more about my plan, I will have plausible information at my fingertips. Meantime, I will manage to keep him at a distance until I can sort the few details I know into solid information.

I have no sooner left my message than my phone

announces Erin's call. I chat with her for a short time, following a stupid chain of clichés in an attempt to let her think all is well and normal. I bring the call to a short ending, reminding her of the stack of homework I am facing on my desk. Within two minutes, she calls back. "What's going on? You haven't got homework yet. School hasn't even started! You're hiding something. I can smell it. You guys getting engaged or something? 'Fess up."

I stumble over my response. I can't continue to play stupid, she knows me too well. "Well, there's a minor glitch. I'm confused. Cliff seems to be involved with some heavy operators, in some money-making deal I don't understand."

"Is it about off-shore investments?" she asks.

"Not that I know. Not even sure if Cliff's involved in any illegal junk."

"Some kind of banking fraud, you think?"

"Not that dramatic."

"Is it really something criminal?"

"Don't know enough to tell you. Banking is the last thing I understand. Take my word, I'll keep you in the loop when I know something, okay? The homework's still in front of me."

"You mean the fake homework. Promise you'll let me know what's up," she says.

"I promise." I hope it will be a promise that's true and worth a friend's trust.

40

I head out in the morning with a destination in mind. I now know a shortcut to *The Silent Bean*. I only hope I won't see Cliff there. I want to talk to Sabina again.

To my relief, she's sitting just inside the shop's doorway, surrounded by some paperwork at a corner table. Several tables are occupied, and the low murmur of conversation comforts me. Our talk will not be overheard.

She looks up when I approach her. She pushes a stack of papers to the side and invites me to sit down. She adjusts her white shirt, tucks it further into her navy trousers. "Looking for more gossip?"

I settle into one of the chairs. "Well, not exactly. I've already heard more than I want to know."

She raises her eyebrows. "About the blonde?"

"No, about Cliff's business. But I can't talk about it, it's supposed to be a secret." I'm hoping she'll beg me to tell her more, but she smiles that enigmatic smile and moves her papers further away on the table.

"There is some recent news," she says, "but I can't prove it. Everything I told you before was the absolute truth, you know, gleaned from a house maid and a couple of her fellow workers who were authentic witnesses." She shifts in her seat.

"But this new piece of gossip is not guaranteed? Tell me anyway." I pretend amusement but I admit to myself that I'm hungry for it.

"It's blowing in the wind, but not likely to be untrue. Sure you want to know?"

"Come on, are you kidding me? That's what I came for."

She rises and carries away some of the papers she has put on the other corner of the table. "Be back in a minute." She calls her assistant to the bar, the quietly handsome bar boy I've met before. She slaps one of the piles of paper in front of him and walks back toward me. He winks at me and settles in to his work.

She scans the tables before she sits and lowers her voice. "There's a serious party at the Grenshaw's this weekend. The Westchester house, not the Saratoga mansion. That's the word from the staff. Of course, it could be the parents' anniversary or some other event, but the smell is somewhat romantic, I'm told."

"Parents can feel romantic," I assert.

"True," she admits, "but I don't get that feel from this couple. Have you seen them together?"

"Sure. Back as far as senior year in college and several visits in the last few years."

"Are they warm and cozy with each other?"

"They're pleasant with one another. No kissing in public but good natured and devoted, it seems."

"Are they warm and cozy with you?"

"Not really, but I don't think they ever were, except maybe when we first met. At that time, they knew he was in love with me, he had told them he had feelings for me. But that was before we all grew up." I laugh in spite of myself.

"You're supporting my theory." Sabina does an open hand gesture that says 'so there.'

"So you think an engagement party?" I force the question as my throat clears.

Sabina bows her head. "I'm ashamed to tell you this sort of thing, but I've gotten to know Cliff better than you think. Perhaps there is no engagement party, we'll know if it happens. The thing about him is that he presents this honest, caring façade, but behind it is a wizard who makes you believe it. Do you understand what I'm saying?"

"I understand it, don't know if I believe it. He's made it clear he cares for me; I think he may love me." I'm reluctant to surrender the image I've lived with so long, despite my own growing awareness.

"He lets you think he's protecting you, he makes love to you with whispers, brings you flowers. Right?"

"Yes, exactly."

"Well, he does love things about you. He loves that you aren't on his social level, and therefore at his bidding. He loves that you're grateful for his attentions. He loves to annoy his parents about your background. He's a teen-ager at heart, you know. And he loves that you open your legs for him with such enthusiasm, because the blonde isn't quite so generous." She puts a hand on my arm. "Is this too painful? Are you angry with me?"

"No, I'm not angry with you. I guess what you say is something I have to consider." For reasons I can't explain, I trust this woman, this friend of Cliff's who was introduced to me as one of his most intelligent and capable clients. "But," I'm led by my uncertainty, "how do you know these things about him?"

"Exactly because of those qualities he admires in me. The closer we got, the more I saw through the façade. I don't mean to compliment myself, but my senses of truth and honor are very sharp, and soon I began to see the core he can't hide, the facade he has perfected, the mask he wears."

"What do you think I should do?"

She stretches and gets back on her feet. "Not much for you to do right now. He'll spill it all the next time you have a real conversation. He may not realize he's revealing anything, but you're a woman. You'll get it on the spot."

I stand, ready to leave. I have to be alone. "Sabina, see you the next time I need to hear good news."

We share faint smiles, and she gives me a pat on the

shoulder as I head home.

I open a lengthy message when I check my phone at the apartment.

Cliff has left me a heap of information. It seems my four-day absence will not be a problem for him, as he also has an unusually full schedule. The weekend in particular has fouled up his timetable, and as a result we will not be able to share the weekend time he would have liked to spend with me. He wonders if I might be available for several nights of the following week, since he so much misses our loving. And he actually mentions several of the techniques that please him the most. If this message were written on paper, I would shred it to confetti. But I'll save the message, to remind myself how Sabina's words line up with the words I'm hearing.

41

I work so hard the first days at school that I feel the girls are teaching me. They grasp every thought, every nuance, and connect it with another that's even more sophisticated. Some of last year's students are still with me, like Becca, Janina and Noreen, all best friends. They have become incredibly mature, no mention of the 'last one in' our class room. Their presence is the luck of the draw, since I share the grade level with another teacher. In any case, new students or old, they amaze me with their willingness and achievements.

Life is back on an even keel at East Harlem Academy. As I leave one afternoon of those early September weekdays, thinking of the girls and humming to myself, I am euphoric. I feel safe in my new apartment, and I love my job. What more is there to ask for? Well, maybe love. But I may have to wait for that.

It has been two weeks since Cliff has come to me, some professional gathering of millionaires having come together in a well-known New York spa upstate. Despite the time away, he has called me daily, assuring his need for me and promising the pleasure of our reunion. I suspect he is enjoying an engagement celebration with the blonde.

In my heart, I know he has to keep our connection alive, especially to protect his relationship with my uncle. It is hard for me to accept this. I can't forget the way he has treated me in the past, how irresistible his advances. There's still a small cup of love to drink from, I hope.

I await Cliff's report about his spa. Perhaps he will

reveal his true feelings for me, or assure me that I'm his only love. Tonight is the first time we've made a plan since the weekend of the party two weeks ago (of which I'm supposed to know nothing, of course).

42

We are curled together like two spoons after a satisfying hour in bed. There has been very little conversation since Cliff came into the apartment, backed me up against the bed, and with some urgency, laid me down on it. He said "Finally!" once or twice as he stripped and helped me remove my clothes. I remain silent, waiting for whatever is to come.

He turns to me. "Missed you."

He sits up, covering our naked bodies with a corner of the sheet. "Really, Kit, missed you as if I'd been in prison."

"It's only been a couple of weeks," I remind him.

"Felt like longer. I thought of you every night and every day. Being in bed without you was torture."

I am determined not to respond to his neediness. Besides, I'm not sure how much of what he says is to be believed. I decide to test him. "So, when will we get together again?"

He swallows hard and clears his throat. "Good question." He runs his fingers through his hair and mumbles a word or two before he attempts an answer. He heads for the bathroom, holding his clothing in one hand. "Be right back."

I get up and dress myself, prepared to hear his speech.

He returns, looking reasonably neat. "It's a little problematic," he offers.

I stare at him, making clear I am not considering this a complete explanation. "I'm sure your schedule's full. The work part of it, anyway. But what about your social life?"

He glances at his watch, and sits on the couch. "Look, you're not going to get this, but give me a chance. My whole life has changed. My job hours are upside down. My weekends are not my own. I can't explain the whole situation, but I hope you'll trust the fact that my time is no longer my own."

He looks to me for reassurance. "Does that resonate with you?" He pats the cushion next to him. "Please. Sit here, please."

I sit abruptly and speak more boldly than I thought I was capable of. I look directly into his eyes. "So you're telling me I'm your weekday girl, coming in second to the weekend girl?"

Shocked and nearly speechless, he stands and reaches out to me. "You don't understand. It isn't like that, you can't know..." He fumbles for words that will save him. "Everything I do, I do for you." Restless, he strides to the other side of the room.

"Like invest in sick deals with my uncle?"

By this time, he's over by the window with his back to me, nervously rubbing his hands together. "Look, I got in deep with your uncle. At some point I met him in Boston and kind of got pulled under."

"Pulled under?" I'm almost screaming but I swallow the volume. "You recognized what was going on there and bought the party ticket? Did you fuck a little girl to see what it was like? And how much of a cut do you get from Seppi and Uncle Frank?"

"It wasn't like that. It wasn't, Kit. I swear."

He comes back to me. He buries his head in his hands. I realize he is crying. "It was all about the money. But I didn't know the price then." He tries to embrace me but I shrink out of his grasp. "Kit, my father..." He stops, and then starts again. "My father and this colleague of his, they planned the whole thing. If I got engaged to Susanne, it would become a family business. Her father is a multimillionaire. He has always wanted her to marry a banker. And he took a liking to me."

He sees my frozen face as I stand. "No, wait, there's more. Mr. Draid has known and worked with your uncle for many years. They meet regularly, they share information, they travel for similar reasons. They keep contact with people you wouldn't believe they actually know." Now he's pouring out information I haven't asked for.

I step out on a limb. "And his daughter?"

"He wants her to be part of the financial world. She has tried it without much interest or success, and so he finally extended friendship to my dad, bringing Susanne to our home, hoping I would find her attractive and bring her into the family."

"Family? As in my uncle's 'family'?"

He actually smiles. "I guess you can call it that. The Draids have the kind of power you can't escape. Not if they need you."

"So you found her attractive?"

"Kit, I had no choice. The pressure from my father, the frequent time spent with the Draid family, the hours accompanying Suzanne on horseback around their property...It was just the kind of luxury and riches I had never seen. My family is financially well fixed, but this was beyond anything I'd ever come across."

"So you are getting engaged, and it's all for the money."

He comes toward me and puts his arms around my stiffened body. I sense he is crying again. "Please, Kit, I don't want to lose you. I can be engaged to her for years, just to mollify her father. I would not let it go further, I'd do nothing beyond that. You and I could still be together." He begins to caress my face and throat. "We could still enjoy each other's bodies, I'd come to you whenever I could, meet occasionally for dinner at some little known bistro downtown, we don't have to give this up."

By now his hands have moved to more intimate places. I am paralyzed with fury and fear. Is this the man with whom I've been sharing my body for months, who seems to have a close connection with my uncle?

I take deep breaths, and push him toward the door. I have more strength than I've given myself credit for. I make eye contact and maintain it.

"It's not happening. I will not be your weekday fuck. I will not listen to tales of you and Barbie on horseback. I will count on you to do the correct thing and get out of my life. And I will not hesitate to report to my uncle anything that I think will hurt you. And to your rich father-in-law to be, as well. Does that resonate, as you so sleazily put it?"

He is unable to face me. I see a few shiny tears on his cheeks. He walks slowly to the door. I pick up his jacket and throw it at him, pleased with the Hollywood scene I'm creating. He opens his mouth to speak, but can't get a word out.

I slam the door behind him. "Wish I had Ginger handy," I whisper, delivering a weak smile to myself in the mirror behind the door. Of course mention of the gun makes me think of Vincent, the subdued locksmith who has left me, to work for my uncle in Canada. I wonder where he is.

Weeks go by. No word from Cliff. I assume he has gotten my message. I think of my foolishness, my belief in his façade, the rich banker who tempts me with travel, who fascinates me with his ability to impress clients, and my slow awareness of his true feelings for me. All he ever wanted, or perhaps still does, was my willingness in response to his sexual needs. I feel as stupid as he is predatory. I was so needy, so damaged, so fearful. I was a perfect victim.

43

It's November and I'm waking up to the beginning of the Thanksgiving weekend. At six in the morning on a holiday Friday, I don't need to fly out of bed, as is my usual rising habit. I count all of the things I'm grateful for, and relax. Lazily, I survey my apartment - its space, its tiny kitchen, the enormous bathroom (must've originally been the small bedroom), the tub with its curly feet. I am happy here.

I'm suddenly aware of an unusual shadow moving on the window. First thought is a good sized bird. I've become familiar with virtually every bird out there since I started feeding them. I've attached a narrow metal tray to the sill, and every day I fill it with seed I purchase at Key Food. This shadow is not a bird. At first I think it's someone's pet gone lost, swinging from a tree branch in the church yard behind my building.

It's early enough that nothing is completely clear; I am suddenly not at rest. I tip-toe over to the window and stand to the side so I am not immediately visible. I peek around the window frame, only to see nothing moving. Nothing or no one is swinging. But wedged stock-still in the crook of the old tree is my former husband, simply sitting now, and staring directly into the apartment.

Trying to put a plan together, I can't think clearly beyond the need to escape. I consider removing my pajamas and getting dressed, but I'm afraid to leave the apartment in any case. I could hit the street but he could possibly see me open my door from his perch, or from the back yard, and pursue me. In a panic, I call my uncle, not even ashamed of my need for his help. His voice is scratchy, and he gives me no opportunity to speak. "What the hell, calling me at this time of day before a holiday? You don't talk to me for weeks, I get to find out from your aunt that you moved, and all of a sudden – Well, so what's the damn reason you have to bother me now?"

"I'm sorry, Uncle Frank. Been so busy with school, you know how it is." I am wet with sweat.

"Yeah, I been busy myself. So what do you need this time?"

"It's Joseph, he climbed a tree out in the yard and he's watching me. I'm so afraid he's going to try to get in. I don't even know how he found me. Can you come over?"

He is quiet for several seconds. "Are you serious? Is this more of your hysteria, another story, fantasy stuff? Joseph's got a job to take care of today, and we agreed he'd do it before dawn. How would he know your address? He couldn't possibly be anywhere near you. And I can't get to you either. I can't do it, Kit. Too much to do before the weekend lands on me like a piece of plywood. Let me think... I got it. Look, I'll send one of the guys over to test the locks and make sure you're okay. Maybe I'll see you Sunday dinner." He disconnects. A minute later he calls again. "Guy's name is Louie, I think. Or something like it." He disconnects again.

I'm wiping tears from my face, shamed by having called him at all, and shaken by my inability to come up with a plan. I sneak on my knees to the window and hope my eyes aren't visible as I get them as close to the sill as possible. Joseph's still motionless in the tree.

He doesn't see me yet, I think, but I fear his surveillance. I back away from the window, cursing that I've never hung opaque curtains. I move into the bathroom, reaching up to the top of the medicine cabinet, which has become the safe place for Ginger since I no longer have a laundry area. Hand shaking, I take the Ruger down. I know it's loaded, but I check to be sure. It's ready to fire, but I can't say *I* am.

Still clinging to the gun, I move slowly to the window. I don't see Joseph now. Realizing that the window is not locked, this because of the daily bird banquet, I move quickly to close the catch. It's difficult to turn. I put the gun down so both hands can work. A sudden idea dawns on me, if a minute late. I should call the police.

Suddenly there is a shower of broken glass that lands on the window sill and the floor. A familiar hand reaches in to turn the lock, unaware it is already unlocked. Joseph begins to push the window up. He is on a narrow ledge below the window, one that allows the window washers to reach windows on my floor. All he has to do is use the bird tray for leverage.

I follow my instinct and pick up the gun. I hold it as correctly as I can in both trembling hands. I back away from the window and wait for him to come into sight. I hear a strange noise at the other window and whirl to identify it. Nothing.

Suddenly I am grabbed from behind. I try to point the gun, but he snatches it from my hand. He has me in a gentle choke hold. I am unable to pull away, I can't face him, I'm having trouble taking deep breaths, although I can breathe.

"Did you ever think we'd get back together, Kit? Ever think we'd be able to fuck each other in a pretty bed, at our leisure, with nobody to disturb us? I've been waiting months for this. I didn't have to sneak into your school, or have the little girls usher me into your classroom, or play any other dirty trick. Want to take a bath first? I'm kind of grimy from my vacation in the tree."

He faces me and has to soften his hold. I loosen my arms and push violently to free myself. I don't get two steps from him when I feel something hit me hard, behind the ear. I go down like a shot deer. I forget for a moment where I am. The pain doesn't surprise me; the dribble of blood goes down my neck. I wipe at it and smear it on my pajama pants. I shake my head to have a better look, but my vision remains unclear. I blink until I can at least see the nearest surroundings.

He is standing above me. He switches the gun to his left hand as he kneels to soothe me. "My poor girl," he says softly, stroking my hair. "Don't make me do that again, I don't want to hurt you. Can you hear me?"

I can hear, if not clearly, but I pretend to hear nothing. I stare at him.

He puts my fingers on his lips, as if he expects me to read his words with my fingers. I close my eyes. "Come on, Baby, we'll take our bath and you'll feel much better." He lifts me off the floor and leads me to the bathroom. Here I am truly fearful, remembering blows I bore from him in a room just like this.

I manage to seat myself on the toilet until he finally allows me to settle myself and urinate. He needs two hands to steady me as I pull up my panties, and I notice the gun is not in sight. I scan the room. I don't see it in the bathroom, and assume it is either in his pocket or on the table outside the bathroom.

Holding me with one arm, he runs water into the tub, checking temperature and depth until he's satisfied. "Okay, let's haul you in." He picks me up to clear the edge of the tub and eases me down into the warm bath. He strips me of my wet clothing and removes his jeans, shirt and underwear. I watch terrified as he sits opposite me in the water, maneuvering space for both of us. It's a tight fit, knees overlapping and bones pressed against the cold ceramic sides of the tub.

He begins to touch my torso, murmuring his wish for us to be together again. I struggle to rise, telling him I have to use the toilet again.

"Damn, woman, you just peed. How long are you going to make me wait?"

"I'm the one who can't wait. Now let me get back on that toilet."

He considers the situation. "This water's perfect temperature. I'm not getting out of it again. Don't need a chill."

"You want me to dirty the water?" I struggle to rise. "Help me to the toilet."

This display of weakness seems to soften him. "Shit! Okay, okay. Hang on, I'll hand you out." He stands up in the tub, lifts me under the arms and puts me down outside the tub.

I slip for a moment on the wet tile floor and lean on the opposite wall. I'm feeling stronger as I realize I have exerted some power. Seated on the toilet seat, I almost laugh, thinking of the weapon I've used to get my way. I double my torso over as I sit, displaying some discomfort and suggesting I'll need some time.

I casually look around this room I'm so familiar with. Not much to help me. There is a plastic toothbrush holder on the sink and a mug for rinsing one's mouth. I look twice. The mug has an old fashioned look, thick and heavy, with a painted flower and a sturdy handle. Can I get my hands on it? Is he watching me every second?

I'll have to move quickly. I reach for the toilet paper. I think of the metal tube that holds the paper, but I cannot separate the holder from the wall. I stand shakily, continuing to show weakness. I turn trembling toward the sink and make a show of washing my hands.

"You're not dirty. Now, come on back to our little love bath." He sounds impatient, but there's an aura of mild humor. When I glance at him, his eyes are riveted to my body, and he is stroking his penis.

At one and the same time, I splash a playful handful of cold water on him, and pick up the mug.

"Hey!" He wipes the water from his crotch. "That's cold! Gives me chills," he says, splashing warm water onto his cold member. He doesn't see the mug come crashing down. I aim for the head, but he turns at that moment and I connect hard with the back of his neck.

Hard enough to make him roar, it seems to have caused significant pain. The mug is in chunks of pottery on the floor. I leap out of the bathroom, heading for my phone and the gun. I snatch up the phone and dial 911 while I am still looking for the gun.

Just as the person on the other end asks for my location, a blow from behind sends me sliding once more to the floor. His anger is flaming. He slaps me in the face with one hand while twisting my arm behind my back.

"Want to make a call? See if you can call me!" He continues to hold my arm while he jams his hand into my mouth. "Go on, call me. Talk to me!" I'm gasping for air and despite my efforts, I'm not able to bite him, his hand is so far into my throat. I am choking.

He takes his hand out of my mouth to touch his neck. "Woman, you give me some real pain." He gently rubs the spot where the mug struck. "That was some power you showed. Been practicing, or what?" His mood has shifted from furious to good natured, although I don't trust it to last. I'm praying for the guy my uncle has sent to check the lock. It's my only chance when Joseph's like this; I've lived through it before but I don't feel I can survive this time.

He starts to tug me toward the bed when he remembers the gun. With a tight grip on my arm, he drags me to the table outside the bathroom, where he last left the gun. My poor Ginger, in strange hands, I think. She has been my safety net without ever being used. Joseph picks her up, examines the chamber and the clip. He feels the heft of it and aims at a bird that has landed on the feed tray.

"What do you think? Could I blow it up with one shot?"

"Joseph, you wouldn't kill some innocent little bird, would you?"

"Maybe not. But you do what I say, or I'll kill you. Got it?"

I nod.

He points the Ruger in my direction. "Okay, bed or tub? You get to pick but I'm going to fuck your nasty butt all day, and if you make a sound... you know what happens."

"Please. Please let's talk. You can tell me again how we can get together, like you said a while back." I move him toward the couch, and I perch on the edge of the seat. "I need to rest for a minute." It's true. I can't even hold my balance.

"Damn! I said pick your spot. Come on!" He tosses the gun at me, tantrum style, just missing my shoulder as it slides to the seat. In the same movement, he slams the lamp off the table. The crash resonates through the apartment, and I stand, startled and hoping to gain some strength.

"How long do you think I'm going to wait for you to open your pussy to me?" He shouts. "You are really heating me up, and I'm pissed!"

He kicks the remains of the lamp across the room toward the door, just as the door clicks quietly open and Vincent walks in.

"Good morning. Everything okay here?" Vincent's voice is soft and slow as he steps over the broken lamp. He looks around the room. "Bit of a mess. Any way I can help?"

"Help? Who the hell are you? Get the fuck out before somebody gets hurt." Joseph is clenching both fists.

"Looks like somebody did." Vincent has seen the blood on my neck and clothing. He takes a step toward me. "Where else are you hurt?"

I shake my head. "I don't know. Maybe nowhere."

Vincent gives Joseph his attention. "Listen, let's all calm down. We can take care of the lady's injury, settle this and clean up the mess. Don't want to see any more blood in here, right?" He half smiles. "Speaking of blood, are you okay, Sir?"

Joseph doesn't answer. All three of us remain still. In that second I come alive. "Vincent, the gun," I whisper, gesturing toward the couch.

Joseph dives for it and turns around, aiming it at Vincent. He loses his footing for a few seconds and recovers his balance to see Vincent pointing a pistol.

Joseph waves the Ruger and screams. "You bastard, spoiling my life and trying to fuck my wife. You don't even know her, and you won't get away with her. She's mine!" He steadies himself to aim and raises his arm to shoot.

The concussion blows through the room. I am deaf. Joseph is on the floor moaning, blood streaming from his thigh, the Ruger yards away.

"Small room for a Glock 19," Vincent says as he tucks his weapon into his belt. I don't recall seeing it there before and wonder where he keeps it.

"Vincent." I can't say another word.

He comes to me and holds me in gentle arms. "What a day," he says. "Just when I thought I was coming to check the lock. Same old game with you, I thought. You surprised me, Kit."

I'm still staring at Joseph's body. Blood is spreading. "What do we do? Do we call EMTs, or the police? Are you going to help him?"

He holds me harder. "Afraid not. I know it seems cold, but helping won't help anything. Too late for EMTs. It's a femoral artery. He'll bleed out before they can get here. We'll call an ambulance. And the police, and your uncle. Meantime, give me a kiss."

"Vincent, what will we do? What about my gun?"

I start to move in the direction of the weapon, and he quickly puts his arm across my body to prevent me. "Has to stay where it landed. Don't touch it, it's evidence."

"But you killed him!"

"Yep, I didn't have much choice." He sighs and pulls a badge of some kind from his shirt. I read NYPD and stop right there.

"You're police?"

"Yeah. Undercover. Your uncle doesn't know, thinks I'm a just a free vagabond who's useful to him. Think I'd go to Quebec for fun? I had to make some connections with the guys who supply your uncle, who volunteered info about a really bizarre story in Boston. Got a pocketful of IDs. Mission accomplished."

He surveys the room one more time. "Nice place, or used to be. And by the way, how the hell did you expect me to find you when I got back? No address, phone's not in service, and I wasn't going to ask your uncle and raise his curiosity. He's funny about that kind of stuff. There'd be an interview, some growling, a speech, and then a warning about staying away from his niece."

He pulls me close. "About that kiss?"

"But you left me, never communicated. I thought you didn't care."

"I can see it now. They'd be tracking my calls and my messages and we'd both be the next targets. And I don't mean the targets at Dino's. Speaking of Dino, he did promise me he'd keep an eye on you, but you didn't practice much. He told me he even called you to encourage you to come more often. Blamed his call on Frank."

"Vincent, where do you go next? Where do you live? How do I keep you close?"

"You're reading my mind. I have a sweet apartment in the Village, it's in a high rise. That's where I'm heading next, and I'm taking you with me. First the details, though. After we get the paperwork here done and submitted, we'll gather your stuff, visit your uncle and invite ourselves to Thanksgiving dinner." The green eyes crinkle a bit. "He's got no family rule against that, right? Your aunts will love me."

He takes me into the bathroom to clean my face. I have forgotten how gentle he is. He stands me in the tub and washes me from top to bottom, checks the bruise behind my ear. "It'll heal. Ugly gash."

He looks me up and down with approval. "You need some clothes. I'll get something from your closet. Jeans and a tee shirt okay for now? Where's the undies?" He steers himself toward the feminine mess in my closet.

He comes back with my clothes and helps me dress. "Looking good as ever," he says. "Let's call the cops and the bus and the rest will take care of itself."

I use my hands to bring his face closer to me, and lean up to caress it. I come closer and whisper into his ear, "About that kiss."

44

We are on Vincent's tiny balcony, fourteen stories above the street, admiring the early light as the sun comes up over the nearest bridge. I love this view. It reminds me of every gorgeous calendar page I've ever seen.

We have just rolled out of bed after a comfortable cuddle. Vincent puts his arm around me after a few minutes of admiring the skyline. "Come on, let's go inside. It's chilly. We'll go back to bed for a while and then we'll go have coffee at *The Bean*. What do you say?"

"Okay, *The Bean* it is," I say. No work today for either of us. For a change the off-days coordinate. Sabina will be pleased to see us; we aren't steady customers but are always welcome. First, back to bed for more snuggling and other intimacies.

It is almost a year since the dreadful day Vincent came to my Brooklyn Heights apartment to check on the lock. We don't talk about it. His part in the event has been investigated multiple times and found without blame. We live every day grateful for our time together and satisfied with jobs we love. It's a blessed way to live.

We arrive at the coffee shop by ten o'clock. Sabina comes by with two luscious warm scones, a pot of coffee and two cups. "Here you go. Don't let me interrupt, but I have something for you to check out." She drops today's folded *New York Times* on the table. "I think it's page seven." She walks away to attend to an elderly woman who asks for tea. Tea, at *The Bean*! We shake our heads as we each reach for the paper.

Vincent sees it first, halfway down the page. He motions me to come closer. The full headline reads: **Boston Pimps and New York Bankers Arrested for Involvement in Pre-Teen Sex Ring**.

The story continues: *Giuseppe Milano and Matthew Corey of Boston are held for allegedly hiring four freshman college students to take part in the assaults of well-to-do pre-teen girls who paid high prices for the sexual activities. Supposedly, the girls wanted to lose their virginity with handsome men. Milano and Corey are being interrogated for their part in drugging twelve- and thirteen-year-old girls with rufi so they would not be able to identify their rapists or recall the experience in detail.*

Investigation has revealed a financial connection to several New York bankers and some known mobsters who invested in the profitable scheme. Several bank VPs, including Clifford Grenshaw and Phillip Draid, are being held for further questioning. No charges have yet been made.

Sabina drops by with our check and tears it up before our eyes. Confused, Vincent reaches for his wallet. "On the house this time," she says. She gives us each a hug. "Don't get used to it."

EPILOGUE

There are some loose ends to be tied, and some knots to be untied.

My uncle was detained for a short time as a result of his close connection with Seppi. However, it was not possible to charge him for any of the Boston events. He had, after all, been at that time abroad, visiting his elderly mother in Sicily, where he also attended an Italian conference made up of old friends who shared his business interests.

After some family infighting and, in some cases downright battling, Uncle Frank finally agreed that Vincent had lived up to family rules by saving my life, and accepted him into the family. But he still refers to Joseph's death as a sad loss, the result of a misunderstanding. I will probably never know what bound them so tightly.

To the delight of all five aunts and Erin, Vincent and I were married shortly after his winning the family's approval. Uncle Frank's gift to us was a sparkling diamond ring, one that he called "the prize of my jewelry business," a business of which I had truly never heard of in my life as a family member. Aunt Concetta, who had wanted me to have money, protection, love and a ring, repeatedly displayed my ring on her own finger, flashing it to Big Tony as an example of what a proper ring should be. Erin later sent a hand-painted card, on which she scribbled "Love is lovelier the second time around – or whatever the number is in your case. BFF, Erin."

Something about Vincent's past troubled me. After keeping it to myself and giving it much thought, I waited for a quiet moment in a west side diner while we were waiting for the counter girl to bring some sandwiches. I finally asked him about Dino's comment that he had "taken down a number of people."

199

"Oh, that. Not to worry," he said. "They're all still alive, if not happy."

"Not happy?"

"Probably not. They're living in places where no one will ever find them."

I must have looked confused.

"Witness protection," he said, and kissed me as if I were lunch.

Thank you for reading.

Please review this book. Reviews help others find Absolutely Amazing eBooks and inspire us to keep providing these marvelous tales.

If you would like to be put on our email list to receive updates on new releases, contests, and promotions, please go to AbsolutelyAmazingEbooks.com and sign up.

About the Author

Teresa Taylor is a teacher, writer and writing coach. She has taught some of the best secrets of good writing, both in the United States and abroad. Since the publication of *Family Matters* in 2014, she has worked harder to master the skills she teaches. She continues to enjoy and take pleasure in her work, and to travel with her husband, Robert Feger, with whom she lives on the North Fork of Long Island.

www.ingramcontent.com/pod-product-compliance
Lightning Source LLC
Chambersburg PA
CBHW050358030726
47503CB00006B/1907